A Journey To Glory

A Journey To Glory

Mark Cornell

A Journey To Glory

& other stories

A Journey To Glory & other stories
ISBN 978 1 76041 280 7
Copyright © Mark Cornell 2017

First published 2017 by
GINNINDERRA PRESS
PO Box 3461 Port Adelaide 5015
www.ginninderrapress.com.au

Contents

Through Amber's Eyes

Giant white heads stretch up into the dark blue sky. Herds of fleecy angels pour over the mountains.

Out on the veranda, high up on a hill, Amber kneels down to pick up her cuddly doll Annie, then stares at the dam wall of cloud bursting in the valley below. Mist marches to her house. Amber hears her mother Emma clanging the dishes in the kitchen sink. The little girl hugs Annie to her face and whispers when ghosts climb over her back fence to circle her garden. The moon's got a rainbow scarf around his neck as he crouches down on her red roof to enjoy the show.

A dragon settles in the shadows of a nearby park telling Amber it's time to go inside. The little girl hears him hissing and watches the flames shoot out of his nostrils. The sun turns pink while he's tucked into his woolly purple bed by a gold stick insect cloud. The little girl shivers when she wonders if the bogeyman's out yet.

'It's tea time.' Amber points her finger into Annie's face and the doll nods her agreement.

As Amber washes her hands, she tells her half-smiling mother all about everything she's seen outside. The little girl suddenly hears a curlew and remembers that Emma told her the call means that a spirit has come down from the sky to deliver a message.

Amber stands beside her ancient wooden family table and peels the crust off the quiche. A candle flickers on the lounge room cabinet illuminating a portrait of Amber's father, Shane. He died of cancer a year ago today.

When Emma and Amber visit, Shane floats up from a crack in the ground to sit on his headstone. Her father is as thin as a rake, pale and doesn't talk very much. He thanked them for the stubby and kept blowing kisses when they said goodbye to him this afternoon.

Amber spits tiny pieces of quiche from the corner of her mouth while she tells Emma of the adventures of the invisible monster Gordon, who lives inside her doll's tummy. Gordon loves to jump off from high places and zoom around the house. The monster does a whole swag of silly sounds like weeing, pooing, farting and flushing the toilet.

Eyes watering, Emma traces her finger around her wineglass and watches as tiny gods rise and fall in the red sea.

After eating six Dutch baby carrots, Amber shuts her eyes and holds out her pink hand for a surprise. Emma places a blue Easter egg in her daughter's palm. Amber opens her eyes, screams then does a little egg dance.

Clouds press their watery bellies against the roof. Droplets create a song. Amber's blue eyes sparkle when she tells her mother that her bottom front tooth is coming loose. She opens her mouth like a baby bird to let Emma inspect her gums. The little girl can hardly wait for the tooth fairy to come and place a coin under her pillow. Amber's woken up in the middle of the night sometimes to watch fairies sprinkle their magic gold dust around her bedroom.

The little mermaid bathes in the deep blue sea surrounded by shining coral and glittering shells. She sees the Prince in his fine sailing ship and wants to marry him. Marriage is easy; all you have to do is stand next to the person that you love. She was married four times this week to her boyfriend Liam at kinder. Her mother tells her to hurry up or she'll miss her bedtime story.

The little mermaid groans as she pulls out the bath plug. Her porcelain limbs are covered in goose bumps when Emma wraps her up in a towel and gives her a cuddle. Amber hears her mother's sniffing and tells her not to cry because Shane will live in their hearts forever. They silently sway together.

Amber munches her bedtime biscuits and slurps warm Milo while Emma reads Hans Christian Andersen; tonight it's the beautifully sad *John's Travelling Companion*. When Amber first heard the story, she had nightmares that a troll lived in the darkness below her bed. She used to run screaming into her mother's room. But she's a big kinder girl now. Amber's two goldfish, Cleo and Waterboy, glide around their green forest and golden castle. The little girl loves the bubbly sound of the fish tank filter; it helps her sleep at night.

Emma turns off the Hey Diddle Diddle lamp and switches the night light on. Her breath is grape fragrant when she sings John Lennon's 'Goodnight' to her daughter. Emma swallows hard while she reflects that Shane used to sing this lullaby to his daughter every night. When people ask Amber what music she likes, she tells them she loves her dad's favourite record, *The White Album*. By the time she was three, Amber could sing all the words to 'Happiness is a Warm Gun'. The little girl recalls the way her father's sandpaper fingers used to pat her off to sleep. Amber hugs Annie to her chest and sucks her fingers. She misses Shane's comforting smell of beer and cigarettes.

The last thing Amber hears is the growl of a possum in the old gum tree outside. The little girl's arms and legs start to twitch. Emma counts her daughter's kicks up to ten; she calls them dream kicks. The mother sits on her stool next to her daughter, studying the innocent face, which mirrors her dead partner. Emma goes back into the lounge room to drain her bottle, cry and listen to the Beatles.

Amber walks along a winding track into a valley then sees a river. It's not like any river she's seen before; it's so deep and blue! The little girl makes her way across rapids and comes to a part of the water that's square like a swimming pool. She still has her clothes on but doesn't care when she jumps right in and dog paddles.

The colours are so different; the bush is light green, the water light blue. A big and strong Shane wades up to her with a beaming face. He's not the skinny skeleton he used to be. Shane tells his daughter to place her arms around his neck and hold on tight. They float down the river together. Her father's shoulders are as big as an island. When Emma asks where they're going, Shane says he's going to carry her all the way down to the sea.

Black Tuesday

One day the sky disappeared. First there was a puff of smoke, and then another and another until a big brown curtain grew over the hill. The sun went red and coughed before it died. Sometimes I saw a yellow flame start up miles away from the big fire, but the brown cloud would get fat and gobble it up. It rattled like a train. A long red snake slithered around the bottom of all the trees.

Everything's gone dark like night-time but Mummy has just picked me up from school. My skin sticks to the back seat of the Morris Minor. I pull my black school shoes off and kick my grey socks on to the front seat. The wind is making the car rock. Come on, Mummy. I want to go home! She says I'm not allowed to get out while she does the groceries. She reckons she won't be away for very long but she's been away for ages. I'm busting for a drink!

When Mummy comes out of the shop with her brown shopping bags, her eyes look like my cat Sooty's did before Daddy ran her over. He backed out of the garage in a hurry to go to work and didn't see poor old Sooty. Sooty's eyes were as wide as saucer plates when the blue van squashed her. The pussy cat must have been made of rubber because the tyre stretched her neck out. Sooty did a cartwheel then the poor puss jumped over our front fence. Daddy got out of his blue van and ran like billy-o into Mr Saxon's front yard and grabbed Sooty by the tail. You should have heard her wail and spit. Daddy checked her out; he's good with animals. He reckons Sooty wasn't hurt at all! I guess it's true what they say about cats having nine lives. I always run out onto the nature strip and wave goodbye to Daddy every morning until his blue van disappears over the hill.

Mummy chucks my pongy socks back at me then speeds home through an ash shower. It's beautiful. Everything looks like it's covered in snow!

'Don't waste water!' the man in the car radio says to us.

All the trees and bushes look droopy, everyone's lawns are brown. Our whole street is full of upside-down beer bottles dug into the garden. Mummy ran up our concrete steps and picked up the black phone. She says she keeps getting an engaged signal. I tell her not to worry about Daddy and try to bring the groceries in but the concrete burns my feet. The wind is like an oven. I'm scared everything's going to melt!

The air stinks. Sparks fall out of the sky like stars. They make me think of the bonfires on cracker night. Everyone comes to the back paddock and they chuck all sorts of things onto a big pile. Daddy always climbs up and tosses the body of Guy Fawkes on top. The guy's made of rags and dressed up in old clothes. I love watching his body turn red and fall apart. The sparks fly up into the stars not down like they're doing now. I can see Daddy nailing a Catherine wheel to the fence and laughing at Mummy being chased around the paddock by a jumping jack. She shouts at me to stop daydreaming and come inside.

Ah! The house is so cool and dark; it's like walking into a cave. Mummy always shuts the doors and windows then pulls down the blinds to keep the stinking heat out. I take off my wet school uniform and lie down in a cold bath. Ah! The water floods my ears until it sounds like I'm in a submarine. I spit out whale spouts then close my eyes and float away like an astronaut in space.

Mummy comes in to scrub my back and wash my hair. I put the flannel over my eyes to stop the soap burning them. I grab her when she goes to pull the plug out. I tell her I want to get a bucket and pour the water all over the garden. Mum's eyebrows go up. She's just taught me to brush my teeth without leaving the tap on. Then I hear the sirens!

I leave puddles all over the floor and stick my head out the front porch to see a fire truck zooming down to the paddock. Mummy, I want to go and watch them! She says it's too hot and dangerous. She starts drying me with a towel and puts powder all over my body. I nag her and start crying until we both go down the street.

The Hawsleys are sitting on their back fence and cheering like it's a footy match. We go down their cracked driveway, past Mr Hawsley's old fruit truck and climb up to take a squiz.

The tallest tree in the world's on fire! His big green head's full of flames. He's bending over to brush them out. Oh! All the yellow grass has caught fire. A big black patch is taking over the back paddock. The smell stings my nostrils. Yuk! Save the tree, Mr Fireman. My favourite hidey spot is way up on top. From up there you can see the whole world! I played hide and seek with Daddy once. He started swearing when he couldn't find me. When he heard me giggling, he climbed up with a rope and tied me to the trunk.

I love the firemen's black uniforms and shiny gold helmets. London's burning, London's burning. Fire! One of them has got a big moustache like a grey broom. He smiles and waves to us and gets his long, long hose out of the red truck. Whoosh. Wow! Die, fire, die! Hiss! Look at all that white smoke! My tree's gone black; there are all these red eyes inside the trunk. Mummy asks him if the fire on the hill is near Daddy's factory. The fireman's got soot all over his face. He shakes his big gold helmet and doesn't say anything. She whacks me a beauty when I ask her if Daddy's going to end up like Guy Fawkes. I see houses popping and cars melting on the hill; it looks like a volcano up there now.

Don't worry, Mummy, I squeeze her hand, Daddy grew up in the bush. He used to swing snakes around his head when he was a little boy. One night he rescued a screaming possum from being eaten by a powerful owl remember? My daddy knows how to fight a bushfire.

Mummy throws down the phone. Her eyes are all bloodshot. She tells me to be quiet and switches on the radio in the kitchen. The man says there's bushfires all around the city. I see a red glow outside the window and wonder whether our willow tree has caught fire. Someone's banging on our front door.

Daddy's standing there with a big smile on his face and Sooty under his arm! He hands my pussy cat to me and hugs Mummy. Daddy keeps laughing, Mummy can't stop crying. He starts spraying the house with the garden hose and I get the bucket and scoop the water out of my bath. I give all our trees and bushes a good drink. Sometimes the wind hits me for six. Daddy's standing in the vegie patch in his white singlet and old shorts pointing the hose to our roof. He gets a bottle of beer out of the van and puts me on his shoulders.

Daddy walks through the smoke and asks me if the teacher read any stories to me today. His hair is all wet and oily. I love his smell. It reminds me of a tree. He wants to know if I can write all the letters of the alphabet yet. I hear all these sirens and see all these flashing lights. The fire sounds like our rubbish truck when it climbs up our street. I nearly fall off Daddy's shoulders when he stops all of a sudden. He goes quiet when he sees the flames on the hill. That long red snake that I saw before has turned into a giant roaring mouth.

Wondering About

The ocean sounds so different down here. Waves hiss as they smash into the stumps of the pier. The foamy swollen water looks like its boiling. I'm a bit scared; I'm used to a sandy sea where the waves sigh, not this freezing dark place full of rocks and seaweed.

Every night, me and my sister Sarah skip down to the pier. The man in the moon trots behind us like a dog. The town lights shine silver trails on the black water. Sarah reckons if you swim out to them, you're taken to another world. She grabs me and tells me off when I try and dive in.

You can see the lights of Warrnambool once you get right out. They glow like a fairy village below the black sky. On a clear day, you can see an island the Aboriginals call Deen Maar. Sarah knelt down and showed me once; I was amazed when I saw this huge flat purple island floating along the horizon. Sarah says the Aboriginals believe that the spirits of the dead end up there. I asked her if she reckons Mum and Dad are on the island. With a tear in her eye, my sister said they probably are because they loved this place. I said we should get a boat and go out and see them. I jump when Sarah yells at me not to be silly, because Deen Maar's surrounded by white pointers.

There's a huge light at the end of the pier that flashes like a giant spaceship. I hear something puffing below the planks. It must be a mermaid, but Sarah reckons it's a seal. Wild horse waves crash against the rocks. Our granddad says each white wave is a warrior returning from the dead.

'My daddy's down there,' says a voice in the dark, so thick that I almost can't understand it.

I just make out a boy's shadow standing on the edge of the pier.

His rod leans against the rail. 'You can see the darling's eyes over there, look!' He points towards the reflection of two blue stars on the black water. 'He used to take me floundering.' The fisher-boy continued. 'You should have seen him jump into the sea to spear fish. Daddy used to shine his torch under the water for me! Oh, the treasures I'd see down there when I was a little tacker! Seahorses puffing their pretty chests out and gliding through the swaying forests…crabs sticking their angry claws up at you while they run sideways! Magical mother of pearl shells. One night, he saw a banjo shark…and waded off with his torch and spear until he was chest-deep in the water. I heard some splashing and saw his torch fall into the water! He called out to me. I'm coming, Daddy, I'd say! Mummy didn't let me go until I bit her arm. My body shook like a leaf when I ran into the water.'

Sarah sniffs. She rubs her cheeks and eyes. I hold my hand up to her and she gives it a gentle squeeze. Her fingers are freezing like a fish. Mountains of mist float towards us. I wonder if we're going to hit an iceberg out here.

'I come and visit him.' The boy drank out of a bottle of lemonade. 'I still see him down there. He's grey now, kelp's growing out of his body, but he's talking to us, hear him?' The shadow put his hand to his ear.

Sarah shakes her head. I hear the sea whisper to the rocks.

'My daddy was a great man. Oh, the stories he told about the whales, the seals, the birds…but then the big ships came along to suck all the life out of the water. The ocean's empty now 'cept for my daddy.' The fisher-boy gives a big sigh.

Sarah shivers as the mist wraps around us like a carpet snake. The spaceship light's being choked by a silver ghost cloud. We race against the fog creeping up the pier. I see the bogeyman out of the corner of my eye!

That night, I dream of a rubbery corpse lying on a seabed, with drifting seagrass hair. Its eyes suddenly open up and stare at me; they are deep blue. Its lips are slowly moving but I have to look away because the inside of its mouth is rotting. I hear him singing then wake up to hear the waves scrape across the beach.

I crawl into Sarah's bed and tell her what I have just seen. She tells me she couldn't sleep. I give her a hug and she pats me on the head.

The last thing I remember is the curtain swaying in the darkness and Sarah's heartbeat.

'You two shouldn't be allowed to wander around the pier at night!' the milk bar lady shouts at me and Sarah the next day. Her voice sounds like thunder. She looks like a tyrannosaurus with that big mouth of hers and wrinkles around her face.

My heart beats like a drum. I hide behind Sarah's back. Why do grown-ups always get angry with us kids? All we want is a bob's worth of mixed lollies.

'Young Gavin Farley and his father drowned down there years ago. He tried to rescue his dad but they were both taken by the sea. They barely found enough of them to place into a coffin. Mrs Farley was put into a loony bin after she heard them struggling in the water.' The milk bar lady bangs her hand on the counter. 'I must speak to that slack grandfather of yours! Your parents are probably spinning in their graves. Here's your lollies, kids.'

I shake like a jellyfish when she hands the white paper bag over to us.

We spend the long sunny day in our togs chasing seagulls and collecting shells on the beach. Sarah makes a seaweed belt for me to hang my wooden sword on. She puts one of Mum's old veils over her head and screams when I rescue her from a sea dragon. After a big swim, I put Mum and Dad inside my fastest Matchbox car and push them off a sandy cliff.

After our tea of chops and baked beans, Granddad tells us he's nicking off to the pub again. His silver beard always stinks of beer and his pipe smoke.

A plover calls out a warning to us when we sneak out of the back window. We see the blue television light in everyone's lounge room while we sneak past their windows. We run past the carnival and get spooked when we hear the mutton birds. We've got the whole pier to ourselves!

It's as clear as a bell out on the ocean tonight. The moon bathes everything in a milky light. You can see the waves coming in for hundreds of miles. Deen Maar looks like a giant white whale.

Me and my sister wait for ages. We watch the two blue stars bobbing on the water but the fisher-boy doesn't show up! I cry and see myself jumping off the pier.

'Don't worry.' Sarah ruffles my hair and grabs my wet fingers. 'There's always tomorrow night, all right?'

When the Sky Fell

Gavin flies through the grey mists of time. The basin of land below him is splashed in neon light. Gavin's brown eyes peer down at the luminous silver snake of a highway. He brushes the top of lamp posts along what used to be a bush track, then hovers over Warrigal Road. Gavin smiles at the ancient word warrigal; it's one of many words from the soil that refuse to be choked by concrete or asphalt.

Gavin gazes up at the stars to spy Bundjel the eagle spirit with his two faithful dingoes at his side. Bundjel once punished an old man who was being cruel to a boy. The old man had grabbed the kid by the hair then dragged him along the ground. The boy's feet carved a gutter in the ground; the boy's tears fell to create the Yarra River. Gavin's dad reckons the eagle spirit threw rocks down from the sky to kill the old man. His father told him that Bundjel's always watching over us.

Gavin stares through a gap in the clouds to make out the red roofs of his childhood. He sweeps down to the front entrance of his family home, Number 2 Nioka Street, then steps back into his eight-year-old body. The first thing he notices is the pong of Actavite in the air. Gavin pictures the huge pink square of the Nicholas factory on the corner of Warrigal and Waverley Road. He recalls how Nicholas used to make Actavite and Aspro. I suppose you need to take one if you have too much of the other, the little boy shrugged to himself.

When he wandered around the grounds of Nicholas's mansion up in the Dandenongs after he got his car, it was like something out of *The Great Gatsby*. Gavin saw ginormous cocktail parties in gardens strung with lanterns where fat red-faced men in penguin suits stood next to laughing skinny women in richly coloured evening dresses and glinting tiaras. A jazz band belted out music from a tent on the front lawn, but no one danced. Moonlight reflected in the eyes of the disturbed possums overhead.

The place is dead now; an empty shell on the side of a hill. The factory's gone too. Yet the eagles still circle the mountain; sometimes they even get down to the suburbs.

Gavin's family knew how to dance. All his relatives loved 'Eagle Rock'. Gavin grinned as he thought how a Melbourne band had a huge hit with a song that paid joyful homage to the most regal of birds. Another balladeer from his hometown sang his last great song about being lifted up by the wings of an eagle. Nowadays you can journey down to the mouth of the Yarra and see a big white statue dedicated to good old Bundjel.

Gavin's jet-black cat Jedda darts up the concrete steps to say hello when he opens the front door. Gavin kneels down to scratch her under the chin. Jedda's motor starts to run as she does a circle dance around his ankles. Gavin puffs into the air and studies the mist of his boyish breath. He feels like a cicada that's shed its shell. He's glad he's put on his thick Collingwood footy jumper that his mum knitted. The boy kisses his pussy cat on the back of her furry black head then hops down the steps to explore the garden bed.

Gavin wonders how his pet praying mantis is getting on. Poor little fella had a broken leg; the boy looked after him in his grandfather's old black toolbox. He filled it with leaves and cotton wool. When he looked better, Gavin let him go in the garden. The tiny head with bulging eyes greets him every morning before he goes to school. The boy's now nursing a moth with a broken wing.

Gavin once caught a budgie down the bottom of his stairs. He was watching *Lost in Space* on the telly when he saw a shadow of a bird fall down from the sky behind the Venetian blinds. He ran to the front door and looked down to see a green and yellow budgie panting away. Gavin raced into the kitchen and yelled to his mum. She gave him a tea towel and told him to walk down the steps real slow. The boy creaked open the front door and crawled down the steps like a panther. He threw the towel over the bird and caught the little bugger! The budgie screamed and bit Gavin's fingers with his sharp little beak as he picked it up and bought it inside. The boy put him in the birdcage with his other blue budgie, Nicky.

Poor Nicky's been looking pretty crook lately; Gavin's mum reckons the old fella's on his last little legs. The green budgie kept his distance. Nicky died a month later; Gavin buried him in the backyard in an old shoebox. When Gavin's mum's tears flooded the ground as he dug the hole, the boy swore she was going to make another Yarra River. She sang for Nicky and prayed that his little soul would soar off to a happier realm. His mum thanked God for his gift from the sky, their new green budgie, who she christened Lionel, after the boxer Lionel Rose.

Gavin walks up his concrete driveway that's been cracked by the gum tree in the front garden. His mum thinks the roots are strangling the water pipes but doesn't want to do anything about it because it's Gavin's favourite climbing tree. It's a foggy morning. Gavin loves the way the clouds have come down to rest on Nioka Street. It's like walking through a huge white blanket. The boy feels as light as a ghost. He loves the way Jack Frost has turned all the nature strips silver.

Gavin steps across the asphalt road to his cobber's house. Danny answers the door in his yellow raincoat and hood. His mum makes him wear it because he can be seen for miles in the fog and won't get hit by a truck. Danny's mum's a strange old bird because every chance she gets she loves to throw Gavin down on the ground and kiss him to death. Her breath always stinks of Invalid Stout, which is fair enough, Gavin reckons, because she's got eight kids to look after.

Gavin and Danny walk up the big hill in the fog. As the freezing air stings their cheeks, they blow on their little boy fingers to stop them from turning into ice. The boys love the way the houses suddenly appear then vanish back into the mist. Gavin points to the white sun sleeping over the middle of their street and swears he sees something moving across its face.

They hear the roar of the rubbish truck and clank of the bins.

The dustbin man suddenly appears out of a cloud with a big smile on his face. He's only wearing his blue singlet and footy shorts. Breath puffs out of his mouth like a steam train. When he sees Gavin's footy jumper, he gives him the thumbs up then points to the Collingwood beanie sitting on top of his head. Gavin loves the way the dustbin man smiles at him every Thursday morning. The boy knows that Magpie people are his tribe. The rubbish truck's light flares in the fog like a UFO then disappears.

Another bloke Gavin loves is the milkman. Sometimes the boy wakes in the early hours of the morning to the clippity-clop sound of the old draught horses pulling the milk cart. He hears the jingly bells on the horses' harness and the clink of the milk bottles as they're dropped off in driveways or front doors. Gavin feels so cosy in his warm bed. The milkman's bells remind him of Santa's sleigh.

Gavin and Danny go past Mr Carmody's house at Number 12. He's a great old fella who makes kites out of balsa wood and brown paper. He uses old rags for tails. Gavin and Danny have spent many a Saturday arvo in the back paddock flying their kites miles up into the blue sky. Gavin's big sister Kitty draws fierce bull faces on the kites with her textas. Mr Carmody visits Gavin's family every Saturday lunch. The old fella doesn't say much, he just sits on the spare blue barstool smelling of beer and smiling at the kids while they knock off our saveloys and baked beans. Dad reckons he likes to get away from his wife because she's a bit of an old dragon.

Gavin and Danny march past Mr Plum's house at Number 18; he's a weird old, bald fella who picks his nose a lot. He flies homing pigeons; Gavin's mum hates them because they always poop on her washing on the clothes line. Danny shot one up the bum the other day with his slingshot. Gavin felt sorry for it when it tumbled down into Mr Plum's front garden. The old codger wasn't home, thank God, or else they both would have been really RS.

Mr Carmody's son Patrick reckons Mr Plum catches cats with a bit of meat in a possum cage then drowns them in the fish pond in his backyard. Patrick reckons you can dig anywhere in the old mongrel's backyard and discover the body of a dead cat. Gavin reckons he's heard them wailing at night as their dunked into the water. He always makes sure Jedda's in at night. Patrick says old Mr Plum was a nice bloke until his only daughter Eloise died in a car crash. She was trapped in the back seat of a two-door Volksy that caught fire.

Dew drops on the boys as they walk past Mrs Swaysland's house on the top of the hill. She's got this giant willow tree in her front garden; it's got a tree house and heaps of swings made from planks of wood and old tyres. The local kids swarm around her place after school. Mrs Swaysland always comes out with a big tray of glasses of lemonade and tick-tock biscuits. She's a grouse old chook.

Gavin and Danny turn right into Armaroo Crescent and go past the old brown-brick hall where the Salvation Army band plays every Sunday morning. Gavin loves hearing the big brass instruments and watching the ladies with the black bonnets making circles in the air with their tambourines. The music sounds a bit like The Beatles latest stuff, 'Penny Lane' and 'Strawberry Fields Forever'. Their new songs remind him of nursery rhymes.

The boys turn left into Bolwarra Street and walk past the milk bar where, if they've got any dosh after school, they'll get a bag of mixed lollies. Gavin and Danny read the headlines out front of the shop. Melbourne's Morris Mini fire bug has struck again. Another Mini's been burnt in the backyard of Mr Frederick Nurks.

'In the backyard!' Danny says to his cobber. 'He's getting bloody cheeky now.'

There's a lane at the side of the milk bar where you can watch the soldier beetles stick to each other. They look really funny because they're always stuck together at the backside and trying to walk away from each other. Danny stands on them sometimes. He's a bit of a boofhead; once he plucked all the legs off a daddy long-legs and cacked himself silly at the tiny bouncing body. Gavin put the poor thing out of its misery.

St Mary Magdalene's is coming up. Their purple uniforms really stick out.

Gavin and Danny shout, 'Catholics are spastics!'

The Mick kids holler back, 'Proddy frogs sit on logs!'

Gavin feels guilty because his mum's a Catholic Her stupid priest excommunicated her when she married Gavin's dad, because he was a heathen. The boy's family dos are always fun because his dad likes to have a few beers and dance with his mum. He calls her the Flying Nun as he spins her around, Gavin chucks off his shoes and socks then joins in. He loves the feel of the dust on his feet. His dad says it's the dust of their ancestors.

Gavin's dad grew up in a tin shack in Murrumbeena. Now he's a foreman in the giant Housing Commission factory. Gavin went there once and saw all these bridge cranes lifting walls and roofs. He got a bit spooked by the men in iron masks using the bright blue welding torches; they reminded him of robots he'd seen in a flying saucer movie.

The boys turn right into Barradine Street and hear the migrant bus coughing up the hill. Gavin and Danny race it to the front of their school, Jordanville South State.

Danny shouts 'Septic!' when he touches the front gate; this means he won't get infected by the germs of the migrant kids.

Gavin watches them pour out of the bus and keeps an eye out for the beautiful Czechoslovakian girl, Emi Major, who always wears red or pink coloured dresses and bows in her golden hair. Gavin gets butterflies in his stomach every time he sees her float through the school gate. The little boy sighs as he recalls how he felt as proud as punch on Anzac Day when he wore his cub uniform and laid a wreath with Emi below the school flag post. He swears she gave him a shy smile.

Brian Hopkins, a skinny little Pommy kid with a mop of blond hair, runs up to say hello. Gavin really likes him because he wears those groovy round wire glasses like John Lennon. Gavin tells Danny off when he slaps Brian hard on the back and knocks his glasses off.

Gavin's never forgotten the day when poor old Brian got the daylights beaten out of him during a game of British bulldog. The mongrels kept pummelling him in the face. Gavin remembers the way Brian wailed when he tried to rub the blood off his broken glasses with his school jumper.

Gavin reckons British bulldog's pretty stupid anyway. The kids split into two sides – the Aussies and the migrants. Even though his family's been here longer than both of them, he's always told to go on the migrant side because he's dark. Gavin doesn't mind; he feels sorry for the way they live in the old army huts down at Gardiners Creek and besides, he knows he's on Emi's side.

All the kids that go before him get bashed up; now it's his turn. The boy breaks out into a sweat as he weaves like billy-o through a crowd of jeering kids.

He gets a knuckle in the face and stares up through his tears to see a giant shadow swooping behind the clouds. It's Bundjel! He screams as he drops a dirty great big rock on the kids waiting to punch him up.

The Back Paddock

'You minimus of hindering knot-grass made'
– William Shakespeare

'We're going to the back paddock to wait for the archangel,' says my sister Maggie, as she lugs the deckchairs over Boofa's fence. Her best friend Julie, Boofa's sister, follows behind her. They're taking Vegemite sandwiches and have got orange cordial in their plastic water bottles.

'What's a…bark angel? A dead dog or somefin'?' Boofa says.

'An archangel! He's the king of all the angels, you drongo!' Maggie says.

'What makes you fink a nark angel's gonna show up to you sheilas?' Boofa says.

'It was on the telly last night: an archangel floated down from heaven and spoke to these girls out in the middle of a paddock. It came to them because, unlike you, they were really good! My blood blister,' Maggie points her pinkie at Boofa.

'Don't point. You'll trip over the fairies.' Boofa laughs at Maggie.

'Good! Last weekend she grabbed me plastic machine gun from me and whacked me over the head with it,' I says to Boofa.

'Hey, little ones, what's happening?' Kerry comes up and stares at us.

'Ah, nothing much…' Boofa says.

We're sitting like two birds on a branch of the willow tree in my front yard.

'C'mon, little Boofy. Something's up…'

'Stupid Julie an' her stupid cobber Maggie have gone over to the back paddock. They reckon they're going to park on top of a hill and squiz at the clouds all day until a march angel turns up, like the stupid dumb girls that they are!' Boofa picks at a scab on his knee.

'Hey, little Boof. Why so many negative vibes? Haven't you been listening to the radio lately? This is the dawning of a new age, Boof my little man. I heard that cosmic story too!' Kerry rolls her eyes and scratches her pimply chin.

'I don't have any vegetative hives, Kerry. Anyway, my dad reckons you hippies are full of bullshit.' Boofa peels the scab off and eats it.

'You have to believe little brothers. Aquarius, Aquarius.' Kerry sings and dances like a weirdo down the street.

'Did you see those bloody flies buzzing around her hairy coconut, Christopher? Jeez, she stinks like an outback dunny. The way she dresses too, it looks like she's thrown a bloody tablecloth over her skinny skeleton,' Boofa says to me.

'She ain't got much dosh, Boof. Her old man's a wino. All her mum ever feeds her is bread and dripping,' I says to Boofa.

'C'mon, do you wanna make some grass knots in the back paddock eh?' Boofa says.

We jump down onto the cracks in the concrete.

'Bloodsucker, look out! Aaah!' says Boofa. He piffs a green dart of grass at me and it sticks to my sock.

'Jeez, be careful, Boof. I did that to Maggie once and she reckons that when you pull the bloodsucker out, the tip gets left behind. It burrows into your skin and makes its way up to your heart, then sucks your blood away until you cark it. You know you have to be careful with me. My mum reckons I've got a heart murmur.'

'Aaah, bloodsucker, look out. Here comes another one!' shouts Boofa.

'Aw don't, Boof!' I jump away from the bloody sharp little green thing.

'One fing you've got to learn, Pisstoffer, is that all sheilas are big bullshit artists. I bet ya a bob that they won't see any arsing angel,' Boofa says.

'All right, you're on,' I say to Boof.

'It's a beautiful day,' the wind whispers to me while she makes the long green grass sway.

Boofa's big dark hairy head sinks below the grass like a black moon. I hear him grunt every time he ties up a grass knot.

'There's not a cloud in the sky,' the magpie sings in an old gum tree, as she sticks her beak up into heaven.

I can see Maggie and Julie's deckchairs up on the hill. I can see the back of Maggie's head. She's got thick red hair like a lion. She looks like she's asleep. But I know she's not, because sometimes she picks up her plastic bottle, pulls the lid off and drinks her cordial. Julie's skinny pale legs dangle down over the deckchair. She looks like a stick insect. Her feet just touch the ground. Julie starts kicking up at the gold sun.

'Ha ha, that'll show 'em,' Boofa says.

We've made a dozen grass knots. We lie on our tummies, make fierce faces and hide like two tigers in the jungle. Our sisters never see us. We wait for someone to come along. We wait for ages, nobody shows up. Poop!

'Let's go back to my place for a Milo,' Boofa says to me.

'Yeah, all right. Then what we gonna do?' I say.

'I reckon we should keep digging the hole to China.'

'Won't your dad tell us off for wrecking his vegie patch?'

'Nah! Ya forgettin' Sunday's the day he takes his truck to the market,' Boofa says to me.

'What'll ya mum say?'

'Who cares? She's inside watching *World of Sport* anyway. North won their first game in a year. Yay! C'mon, I reckon we can reach the other side of the world by teatime,' he says.

We go into Boofa's dad's shed, find some shovels and start digging away.

Big grey clouds march over the sky like giants. Our hole's at least a foot deep by now. I think of what we're gonna say to the first Chinaman we ever meet.

Boofa gets the hose going. He fills up our hole, so that the dirt'll be softer for us to dig. We chuck in some leaves and play boats. I wonder if we're gonna fall out of the hole once we've made it to the other side of the world.

The sun's going to sleep behind the clouds. We slosh out the mud with our shovels then hit hard white dirt that looks like a skull. It's bloody hard to dig now, bugger it! Boofa and I throw our shovels on the ground. I wanna go to the back paddock now to see whether the archangel has turned up or not.

'Let's go back to the back paddock, Christopher,' says Boofa.

ESP! It's amazing how many times Boofa reads my mind.

A ray of sunshine breaks through the clouds when Boofa and I climb the fence. Then another and another, till it looks like a humungus yellow spider is dangling over the paddock. A sunbeam shines on something coming towards my sister Maggie. Boofa and I stay on top of the fence. I half close my eyes to make out what looks like a white sheet sailing up towards the girls on the hill. A ghost! I hit Boofa on the chest. He hits me back. He's got eyes like a frightened rabbit.

The wind whooshes. Ah, that's it! The wind's blown someone's sheet off the clothesline. No…hang on a minute. Whatever it is has got long gold hair! It's got pale skin. It's wearing a long white gown. Its feet aren't touching the ground! The wind makes the long grass lean over. It looks like hundreds of green slaves are bowing over to this thing. The grass knows something. My sister knows something.

'The archangel! The archangel,' shouts Maggie as she and Julie jump off their deckchairs and kneel to the white thing coming up the hill!

The wind is blowing hard now. Me and Boofa hang on to each other for dear life. Maggie and Julie are praying now as the archangel floats to the top of the hill. It's nearly there now!

'The archangel! The archangel! Boofa, the archangel. Look!' I shout to my mate.

'That ain't no archangel, you dickhead!' Boofa pushes me away from him.

'Bloody hell!' Someone shouts from near the top of the hill.

I watch Kerry trip over one of our grass knots. Boofa falls off the fence cacking himself, laughing like the mongrel that he is. Bugger it! I've lost a bob!

Murray

I like to float on my back in the river and stare right into the sun. There are all sorts of suns, you know. There's the oven sun, hogging the yellow sky. There's the dragon sun, puffing out giant brown heads of smoke. Then there's the ghost sun, drifting behind sad, grey clouds.

I can feel the earth flying through space when I'm on my back. It soars like a stone flicked from a huge slingshot. I see beelines when I half close my eyes. My river's full of beelines. They hang down from the tops of the trees like big steel cobwebs.

Dragonflies use my belly as a helicopter pad. Sometimes when I'm hungry, I keep my eyes above the surface and suck in water from the fresh river. I let the dragonflies fly in circles around me, then spit them out of the sky and eat them. They sort of taste like crunchy peanut butter.

When I was little, I carved my neck with blade marks to make gills. It didn't work, though; my neck stung when I stuck it into the water and tried to breathe through my red gills. I sank like a rock to the bottom of the water. I love it deep down; there's no sunlight, no noise, and no people with their silly talk. I hate the gasbags who keep saying they feel sorry for me because I couldn't breathe when I was born.

I know how to hold my breath forever, so I can explore the dark caves water and wrestle with the slimy, swaying reeds. I meet my best friends in the riverbed in summer. They sink down from the top of the river like golden blobs of sunlight. They've got long yellow hair. They have tea parties at midday, to celebrate the cool currents coming down from the mountains. My friends make flutes and drumsticks from bones that lie at the bottom of the river. I love to dance and sway to their music! They play songs that sort of sound like watery church bells. Sometimes a giant cod floats by to brush my hair.

When I come back home, I know I've been away forever because Mum's grown more wrinkles.

I like to put hooks on the end of a rope and tug at them with my mouth. One day, a rude old fisherman sprung me and asked me what I was doing completely starkers in the river, with a hook in my mouth and tugging away at a rope. I said I wanted to know what it felt like to be a fish when it was caught at the end of a line.

I like to lie at the side of the river, flap my arms, do somersaults and see what it felt like to drown in oxygen. I float up to the sky when I'm dying. I can see the whole river. It looks like a white ribbon when it's born in the snowy mountains. It grows brown and fat when it meets the sea, like a belly of a snake that's eaten a calf. I turn silver when I float above the earth. No matter how high I fly, I'm safe, because I'm attached to the river by a long silver cord that comes out of my belly button.

I go to the local tip, get bits of clothes and junk, take them home and Mum helps me make dress up fish costumes. My mum takes photos of me in different costumes. See look, there's me as a rainbow trout, a redfin and an eel. My best picture is me posing as proud as punch with a big beaming smile. I've got my goggles on, and I'm puffing my cheeks out like a Murray cod.

My dress-ups are becoming more and more fancy. I can cover up every bit of my body now with my new skin. Mum's really good these days at making fins. I'm good at making huge fish mouths. I use everything from the tip, bits of old tyres, plastic rubbish bins, plastic milk bottles for floaters, old leather belts and rope to hold things together, vacuum cleaner pipes for breathing, bottle-top lids for scales. You name it and I'll use it. Mum, with her head down, spends ages on the sewing machine. I sometimes hear her all night when I try to go to sleep.

Jesus, I hate the magpies! They dive-bomb me sometimes. They scare the daylight out of me when they swoop and rip out bits of my body with their beaks and claws. Every chance I get, I slide up the gum trees and wreck their nests. I hate the way magpies shriek. Birds are the enemy, you know!

My last costume was the best. Mum and I spent days on it. Mum made most of it out of rubber. I'd put on my costume, crawl up to the mirror, and then send it back to the sewing machine, until it fitted perfectly like a diving suit. Mum made fins that stuck out of the side of my new body. My legs squeezed into a big tail. I didn't have arms or legs any more. Mum put a great big rubber fin on my back. I loved to lie on my tummy and watch it as I made it flap form one side of my body to the other. My new fish skin was all grey.

I spent forever in the river, bubbling along brown valleys, then zooming between rocks and logs with my new body. I ignored the stones tossed at me by the savage kids. I had more important things to do; I was hunting yabbies. Then I thought I heard thunder, but it was the loud laugh of one of the idiot kids as he heaved a huge rock right on top of my head. I didn't mind, though. I felt like I was dreaming. I started to suck water through my gills. I felt so warm. I drifted towards the shades. I saw the whole river again. So warm! Everything gushed out of my head. I'd finally become a fish at last!

Use Your Kidneys

Owen was being snarled at. He knew the mouth well. There was a gaping hole in the front because its owner decided to blow on grog the money his parents had given him to fix his teeth. The gap itself was rumoured to have occurred during a stolen car crash. The yellow teeth were well lubricated with spit. Owen had wiped sticky globs of this spit off his face and uniform several times.

Owen William's problem was that he couldn't take the game they were playing seriously. For starters, there were no goalposts. The goals were school bags, which were hard to make out because they were low on the ground and hidden behind a gaggle of boys. Owen chuckled at the mass of writhing bodies that had just grunted, elbowed and kicked their way towards him. Somehow the ball trickled out of this mobile mound of flesh straight into his swooping arms. He turned and aimed for where he thought the school bags were. Owen thought he'd scored a goal but soon discovered he'd kicked the ball out of bounds because he was surrounded by a hoard of abusive boys. Owen leant over to rub his knees and broke out laughing.

Lee 'Ebbo' Evans clenched his fists and circled Owen like a hornet. One thing Ebbo never seemed to be was serious, especially in front of the teachers. He was known throughout Blackwood College for his savage humour. Surely he'd see how silly this game really was, Owen thought. But a grimacing Ebbo stepped straight in front of him.

Owen raised his head and smiled; he held up both of his open hands and pretended to surrender. Ebbo punched the smaller boy several times in the face. A stunned Owen reeled away from his adversary. The tears of laughter on his cheeks turned to trickles of sorrow. The teacher blew the whistle and the ball was kicked back in. A sobbing Owen was left to himself in the middle of the ground.

The boy walked home rubbing his stinging cheekbones.

Owen stared through red eyes into the bathroom mirror and saw a black egg sprouting from the side of his pale face. He placed a flannel under the cold water tap, gasped as he applied it to his bruise then lay down on his bed. He heard a meow through his sniffing. Suddenly his black and white cat Guinness pounced on to his lap. Owen scratched the cat's ears and chin; her lawnmower purr lulled the boy off to sleep.

His mother Rose looked dismayed when he explained the black egg on his face that night at teatime. His father Kevin guffawed over his chops and baked beans then disappeared out into the garage to tinker away on his hobby radio. Owen shuffled back into his bedroom with Guinness, then put his head on the pillow and listened to his trannie. He spent that night twiddling the dial in search of a song that would comfort him.

Owen floated off into his own fantasy world where he was the lead guitarist and chief songwriter of his band. The boy closed his eyes to picture his closest mate, Neil Brown, pounding away on the piano. Owen had a pile of exercise books under his bed containing his own weekly top forty based on the number of times he heard a song. Neil rang every Sunday night to see who'd made it to number one.

He told his mother the next morning that he wasn't going to school.

Rose didn't argue with her son and got into her Morris Minor to go to work. Owen spent most of the day in the backyard under his favourite oak tree, listening to the music on his trannie and watching the cumulus clouds sail by. The boy recalled when he was a toddler how he used to love sitting on his mother's lap out on the front porch and describe to her the shape of the clouds. Owen pictured the imaginary puffy white whales and dolphins that soared over his red rooftop. He remembered the way Rose used to place her chin on the crest of his head and how she always sang to the music on the radio. Nowadays, Rose Williams ran around like a headless chook.

Owen traced his fingertips up and down the backbone of a dozing Guinness. The cat's dreaming green eyes slowly closed. Her black tail lazily flicked below the gentle blue November sunlight. Owen loved the silence that blanketed his suburb during the middle of the day.

Towards the end of the week, the black egg had nearly disappeared. Rose told him it was time to go back to school. Kevin lectured over his shepherd's pie and peas that his son should stand up to the bullies. Owen replied that he was sick and tired of getting the shit beaten out of him every day.

Like all teenagers, Owen was prone to exaggeration. However, he wasn't this time. Ebbo's mates, Lee 'Ant' Anthony, Neville 'The Devil' Whitlow and Graham 'Sexy' Saxon all loved to knuckle him as well. Ebbo and his mates had imposed a reign of terror throughout Blackwood College. The fat kids had been ridiculed and spat at into humiliation, the weak only required one punch in the face and the creative were ritually poofter-bashed. Owen came under the latter category because his English teacher regularly asked him to stand in front of the class and read out his stories. Owen loved to see his fellow students cacking themselves silly over his crazy science fiction stories.

Neil 'Chuck or Charlie' Brown rang Owen Saturday morning and invited him to stay at his place for the weekend. Owen threw his toothbrush, an exercise book and change of socks into his school bag and zoomed off down the street on his pushbike.

Owen and Neil spent Saturday afternoon in the sandstorms of North Africa locked in a fierce battle between the Afrika Corps and the Rats of Tobruk. Neil had a model toy collection of practically every ship, plane or tank built during World War II. The boys negotiated rules only understood by themselves then engaged in an elaborate conflict in Neil's bedroom where Owen's Rats of Tobruk stoutly defended the bed all afternoon. However, the Rats uncharacteristically had to concede defeat after an overwhelming blitzkrieg was jointly launched from the carpet and desk by Field Marshal Ernst Von Brown.

Later on at night, Neil leant up from his bed to tell Owen he was just putting the stereo on. Owen watched from his mattress and blankets on the floor as Neil placed his transistor into a large glass on the cabinet beside. Owen chuckled when the Bee Gees suddenly sounded louder. Neil leant back and sang in a croaky voice to the ceiling.

> Run to me whenever your lonely
> Run to me if you need a shoulder
> Now and then you need someone older
> So darling you run to me.

Owen noticed that his friend's voice was breaking and wished his would too. Maybe with a deeper voice Ebbo and his mates would leave him alone. Owen shrugged. The mongrels rarely physically intimidated Neil when he was at Blackwood College. His friend was a year older than Owen, pushing six foot, and always had a witty reply to whatever garbage Ebbo and his mates dished out. Nevertheless, Mr and Mrs Brown were concerned enough about the level of violence to place their son into another school. Owen missed his friend chronically.

The two boys chatted and listened to an Elton John special until the early hours of the morning. They adored the haunting anthem 'Funeral for a Friend'. Neil mumbled that he was saving his pennies up to buy *Goodbye Yellow Brick Rd.* Sometimes in between songs they heard the crackling sound of the Ashes wafting down the hallway from Mr Brown's radio. At long last, the Aussies were starting to give the Poms a run for their money. They even had a hit on the radio which Owen loved chanting, called 'Here Come the Aussies'.

Sunday was traditionally family day in the Browns' household. After breakfast the family sat around the kitchen and chatted about what they would like to do. Owen loved Mr and Mrs Brown's Scottish accents and admired the way they talked to their children on an equal basis. Neil was the oldest of four children; he had two brothers and a sister. Owen had an older and younger sister who existed on a separate planet. His older sibling hogged the phone, gas-bagging about boys; his younger sister was permanently immersed in a melodrama.

The Browns decided to go to the Blackwood Hotel for a counter lunch. Owen's heart raced; he'd never stepped inside a pub before.

Mr Brown went into the family lounge room to read a book for the remainder of the morning. Owen's blue eyes widened; except for a meal, his father never relaxed in the house during the day. Neil suggested they follow him in to play a game of chess.

'Your dad won't mind?' Owen raised his red eyebrows.

'Nope, not if we talk softly.' Neil shook his blond head.

Neil bit his fingernails and Owen crinkled his brow as an epic cavalry battle broke out in the middle of the Brown household.

'It's all about strategy, Owen…you're getting better at this, by the way. That line of pawns you've put up is nearly impossible to penetrate… Hmm, let's see.' Neil decided to bring out his heavy artillery, the queen. He'd recently taught Owen how to play chess and now relished the challenge his friend was putting up. 'Like the barbarians you're dealing with at Blackwood, it's all about cunning.' Neil scratched the bum fluff on his chin.

'How do you mean, Chuck?' Owen tentatively brought his bishop out.

'Ebbo and his mates have the intellectual depth of a tadpole pond. There's no way of beating them physically, so you have to learn to use your kidneys.' Neil pointed to his temple.

Mr Brown smiled to himself.

'Believe me, I've been racking my brains for ages for a way to outwit those dropkicks but I just can't think of anything.' Owen's eyes misted over.

'Well, don't despair, Owen. We'll nut something out. Check!' Neil grinned like the Cheshire cat.

'Poohead!' Owen's king scampered to safety.

Owen and the Brown family sat out on the back veranda at the Blackwood Hotel. Bellbirds pinged in nearby gumtrees; a swollen Yarra flowed below a hazy golden sun. Owen and Neil stared out towards the red chapel spire of the old monastery. Owen told the Browns he rode his bike down there once and looked across the river to see a couple of priests in their black robes go-go dancing to groovy music blaring out of their trannie. Encouraged by their laughter, Owen chattered away the afternoon, knocking off several raspberry lemonades and savouring every mouthful of his Wiener schnitzel and chips splattered in red sauce.

Kevin snorted over his beer and sausages that night when Owen raved about the huge counter meal Mr Brown had shouted him. He yelled at his son that he expected him to go to school tomorrow. Owen had butterflies in his stomach when he took his Sunday night bath. Neil attempted to ring his friend but kept getting an engaged signal. The boy studied the television guide and smiled to himself when he saw that *Love Story* was coming on at eight-thirty.

The Williams family groaned in the lounge room when the phone rang during the opening credits of the Sunday night movie. Owen came out his bedroom with ink stains on his fingers and picked up the receiver in the hallway.

'So who made it to number 1?'

'John and Yoko, "Merry Christmas War is Over". God, I love that song. If you think of it, Chuck, that nightmare of a war could really be over for good, eh? With us and the Yanks pulling our troops out of Vietnam…maybe the stupid Yanks have finally learnt a lesson and will butt out of other people's wars.' Owen pulled his dressing gown knot tight.

'Speaking of peace, Owen. I think I may have come up with a strategy to stop those trogs from punching you up. Are you going to school tomorrow?'

'Yeah, I suppose…the old man's nagging me.' Owen stared down at his slippers.

'Try bandaging one of your wrists, then when you get to school spread it around that you've sprained it and you're in a fair amount of pain. That's why you've been away for a week.'

'Do you reckon it'll work?' Owen scratched the back of his head.

'I went to primary school with those cavemen. Believe it or not, bullies do care about what other people think of them. How do you think it would look if they starting punching up a kid who's got a sore wrist and can only use one hand to defend himself? They'd reveal themselves for the cowards they really are!'

Owen drew back his curtains to discover silver rings around the full moon. He wondered if the Apollo rockets had left them behind. The boy gave a deep sigh and looked at his alarm clock. It was eleven o'clock! His mind chattered and the butterflies in his stomach wouldn't go away. Guinness leapt on his windowsill to scratch the fly wire screen. Her moonlit eyes flared like headlights. Owen opened the window; his cat uttered a small burr sound as she brushed past his cheek. The boy settled back into his bed while Guinness melted into his side. The last thing the boy heard was Guinness's Volkswagen purr and 'Strawberry Fields Forever' whispering out of his pillow.

Owen barely touched his breakfast. Kevin shook his head when Rose bandaged her son's wrist. Four boys ran up to him when he walked through the school gate towards the portables.

'Where the fuck you been, poof!' Ebbo started to gargle up some spit.

'I had an accident. I sprained my wrist.' Owen held his bandage up.

'Wanking yourself again, poof, eh?' sneered the Devil.

'Actually, I fell off my bike.'

Owen attempted to walk past the four boys but Ebbo blocked his path. Sexy Saxon spat on the ground in front of Owen as a crowd of children gathered around them. Owen stood rigid while his heart raced. Ebbo dribbled spit from his mouth and stared hard at the bandages. The Devil leered then flicked his bony fingers at his victim's face.

Owen jerked his head back and groaned. Some of the children watching began murmuring to each other.

'What are you fucking looking at?' Ebbo spat at the closest onlookers.

A handful of girls covered their faces and screamed. The school bell went.

'As soon as you take that fucking bandage off you're gone, poof!' Sexy Saxon poked Owen hard in the chest.

The children trickled towards the portables.

Owen and Guinness went to bed early that night after a long conversation with Neil on the phone. The boy continued to stand up in front of his class with his bandaged wrist and make children laugh at his crazy stories. Due to his injury, he wasn't allowed to play sport for the last three weeks of term. John Lennon remained number one on Owen's top forty throughout that long summer.

Astro Boy

'Everyone on this planet has a spirit which leaves your body and travels to an astral plane. As you soar off, there's this cord that connects you to your body back on earth. It comes from your belly button.' Joe flicked back his long black hair and took a drag on his strawberry-flavoured cigarette.

'What's an astral plane?' Stephen asked, lying nearby in the shadows on the grass. With his dark hair flowing over his ears and big brown eyes, my best mate looked like a hound dog.

'A higher and more perfect plane of existence where there's no war or conflict of any kind. When you go there, your cares shed like an old skin.' Joe squatted down on his ankles to blow his smoke up into the powder blue November sky.

'The cord you were talking about, is it silver?' Marty's blue eyes focused on the white branches of our smoking tree.

'Yes! How the bloody hell did you know?' Joe's dark eyes widened in amazement behind his glasses.

'I was working for a supermarket once, unloading delivery trucks. One of them didn't see me when it backed into the loading bay and pinned me against the wall.' Marty's large stomach expanded as he took a deep breath and stroked his blond-bearded chin. 'I was crushed and rushed off to hospital. I remember floating on the ceiling and looking down at the operating table as they tried to resuscitate me. I saw a cord drifting up towards me from my body. The surgeon reckoned I was dead for at least ten minutes.' Marty sat on a log shaking his fair curly head, while the rest of us kept silent.

I looked over to Stephen; he probably had the same thoughts running through his head as me. Far out! To think Marty had taken the ultimate step and lived to tell us what it was like! We younger ones always respected Marty and Joe's opinion because they'd both been out in the big wide world; Marty worked as a landscape gardener for a couple of years, and Joe, the lucky mongrel, had been on a year-long holiday to Italy with his family!

Mr Fowler, our social science teacher, marched down the hill towards us. With his long black hair and beard, he bore an uncanny resemblance to Charles Manson. 'Any of you fellas got a spare fag for a dying Spartan?'

'What flavour would sir like?' Joe stood to pull out his silver cigarette case and reveal the fruit-flavoured cigarettes he'd made with his little red plastic roll-your-own machine. The guy had style. He was into Bowie and was an ace surrealistic painter.

'Hmm, let me see…how about banana?' Mr Fowler took out a yellow cigarette and lit up. 'Hmm, delicious! Please don't let me interrupt, boys.' He slid his hands in his jeans pockets and leant against our tree.

'Is it possible to astral travel without actually dying?' I noticed the gleam in Mr Fowler's eye when I asked Joe what I thought was a probing question.

As the smoke curled through his bushy beard, I recalled how our teacher said that he always found the company of 'the blobs' stimulating. The blobs was a nickname he'd coined for us because he said we always enjoyed lounging around and asking the big questions of life.

'I used to do it all the time a couple of years ago. It was grouse! I'd leave my body, meet my mates at Shopping Town and we'd have jumping competitions off the roof.'

Joe tapped his cigarette ash onto the ground.

'How do you get your actual spirit to leave your body, Joe?' I scratched my thick sideburns, ignorant of why Mr Fowler was chuckling away to himself. I was proud of my muttonchops; they were my passports to getting into a pub, even though I was only sixteen.

'Make sure it's absolutely dark and quiet. The slightest distraction could make you miss getting back into your body and end up in limbo!'

'Ooooh!' went the blobs around him.

'Take a series of short sharp breaths, push your stomach out as far as it'll go and keep chanting to yourself, "I will astral travel, I will astral travel." It'll take a while but you'll find yourself leaving your body. Now comes the tricky bit: ignore the demons.'

'Demons!' My voice slipped out like Mickey Mouse before I had the chance to make it sound deeper.

'Demons, monsters, imps: they represent your innermost fears and they'll keep you stuck on earth. Have nothing to do with them or you'll never leave your body and experience the ultimate trip!' Joe pointed his finger up to the heavens.

Mr Fowler challenged me to a bet me that I couldn't do it. I hesitated for a second but a guttural chorus of 'Go ons!' from the blobs, made me get up from the ground and firmly shake my teacher's hand. We bet big money, five quid!

The bell rang and Mr Fowler ushered us back into his class to discuss the Constitutional Crisis. Much as I was pissed off with what was happening to poor old Gough, I couldn't get my mind off the idea of zooming off to a better world. I mean, let's face it, this one sucks! What with the Americans losing a war they shouldn't have fought in the first bloody place and conservatives scaring the shit out of everyone to get back into power! Besides, practically every talk the blobs have these days always goes back to the terror of the mushroom cloud hanging over our city.

'I will astral travel, I will astral travel, I will astral travel,' I murmured to myself that night in bed while I panted. 'Ha! Nothing's happened yet. I will astral travel, I will astral travel, I will bloody well astral travel! Hmm. Joe's right. I'm feeling as light as a feather.

'Yap! Yap! Yap!'

'Shit a brick and fart a four be two, the neighbour's useless fleabag!' I groaned as I slammed my bedroom window shut. 'I will astral travel, I will astral travel, I will astral travel,' I chanted and pushed my stomach out. A picture came into my mind of Joe and his mad mates cacking themselves silly as they bounced over the suburbs with silver cords dangling out of their bellies.

During Mr Fowler's class the next day, Stephen reckoned he'd left his body and waited for me on the roof of Shopping Town. When he realised I wasn't showing up, he floated over to New York and got stoned with John Lennon. Stephen reckons it was the most cosmic experience of his life, bugger it!

I tried to astral travel even harder that night and then, an amazing thing happened. I was chanting and feeling my body float up from my bed when I sensed a presence on my desk.

I told Joe about it the next morning as we smoked below our ancient gum tree at the back of the school. 'I was leaving my body when I suddenly sensed something sitting on my desk. I kept my eyes closed and kept chanting but the thing wouldn't go away. An image of a body wrapped up in bandages slowly appeared in my head. It was freaky, I tell you! It looked like an Egyptian mummy!'

'Yep, that's your fear, all right, Paul. Fight it and ignore it!'

Joe offered me an orange cigarette but I took a blueberry one instead. Yummo! His fags are so moreish! Joe gets that extra tang by using fruit flavoured rollie paper and filters.

Mr Fowler stood above us with a grin from ear to ear. 'Try and ignore it,' he says.

Easier bloody said than done. That bloody thing in my bedroom's spooking me! Every night I chant and feel light-headed, and then this creature all wrapped in bandages leers out of the dark at me while Stephen's getting it off with a rock star. The turd rang me up the other night to tell me that he'd bonked Stevie Nicks!

Mum noticed my nocturnal chanting one night and came into my room for an explanation. I wasn't embarrassed because she's the sort of person you can chat to about these things. She's a Catholic, you see. I have this theory that because they're forced to think about the big issues of life when they're young, you can talk to a Catholic about anything spiritual.

As I explained the whole astral travelling bit, Mum's eyes turned into the shape of saucers. She was weirdly silent for a week and I noticed that when I came home from school my bed wasn't being made any more.

Then the old man came into my room when he heard my mantra, bugger it! 'You've got to stop this bloody astro travelling garbage, Pauline.' (My dad calls me Pauline because of my long red hair. I've got two sisters; Dad thinks he's being funny when he introduces me to people as his third daughter.)

'It's *astral* travelling! Not bloody *astro* travelling! Astro's the dog from George Jetson.'

'I don't care what the bloody hell it's called, you've frightened the daylights out of your mother. You never think of her feelings, do you, eh? She's home by herself in the house all day and she's too scared to go into your room because of that bloody mummy! Just stop doing what your long-haired friends tell you to do, will you, or else!' Dad stormed out.

'Or else' was usually a clip around the ears, so I paid five quid to a beaming Mr Fowler the next day.

Thus ended my only attempt to leave my body without the aid of a substance. Not long after, I started walking through the streets of the city protesting, and studied at university in search of a better world. But I guess there's only one way to find out if there's a greater existence beyond than this one, and that's Marty's way.

Years later, I was to find out his story was complete bullshit too.

The Min-Min Light

Amy was anxious in the dark. The occasional beam of light from an oncoming truck lit her face. She was as still as a statue, but her eyes gave her away. Those hazel eyes, which Richard knew intimately, were moist and staring out to the night sky for reassurance.

She hadn't spoken for ages. When Richard took his hand off the steering wheel to find hers, Amy flinched. Normally she'd wrap her hands around his fingers then rest his hand on her lap.

'What is it, Amy, eh?' Richard glanced at her silhouette leaning against the car door. He found her cold fingers to give them a gentle squeeze.

After a long pause, she replied. 'There are no towns! I haven't seen a house for miles. I can't handle this nothingness.'

Amy's plaintive voice shocked him; she'd sounded so different an hour ago when she marvelled at the sunset over the desert. Richard recalled the way the cloudless sky flared purple as the mobs of wallabies grazed by the side of the road. The air around them had teemed with flocks of shrieking cockatoos and corellas. When Amy spoke of a blue mountain range basking on the horizon like a goanna, Richard hoped she shared his love of the land.

But night came; Amy flicked the dial of their car radio, only to get static. 'Can we please stop at the next town, Richard?'

'Didn't we say we wanted to get to Adelaide tonight?' Richard remembered them clinking their glasses in agreement at the pub back in Dimboola. 'There's miles to go yet. We've got at least another four hours' drive, I reckon. We haven't even hit the border!' His face flickered red in the blackness of the cabin as he lit a cigarette.

To Amy, even though the car droned away at a hundred miles an hour, it felt like they were stationary. She pictured them as two specks of light in an ocean of black.

'It's so beautiful out here, Amy! Just think, we're miles away from the madness of the city. I mean, look at those stars!' Richard pointed to the white haze of stars stretching across the windscreen.

Venus blazed near the horizon like a silver beacon. The Southern Cross soared along the backbone of the Milky Way. A silent Amy clutched Richard's hand as he brought it back down.

'You've been out in the bush before, haven't you?' When Richard wound his window down, the desert flooded their cabin with a moist fragrance.

'Not out here, not in the middle of the night!'

The fear in her voice touched him. He knew that feeling well. His mind went back twenty years to the first time he camped with his parents. He was five and loved the novelty of an open fire but was horrified by the wall of black that surrounded him in the tent when he was tucked in to sleep. The boy howled with the certainty that a monster was waiting for him in the dark. He never forgot his mother's face in the torchlight when she growled at him.

It took Richard years later, when he was on holidays from uni, for him finally to overcome his terror of the dark. His hippie friend Peggy had a farm down in Tasmania. She encouraged him to skinny dip with her in the King River. Richard never forgot the night he and Peggy stood arm in arm to study their reflection in the water. He felt every fibre tingle in his body when he saw their merged outline below a forest of stars. As Richard peered into this mirror of the constellations, he learned he was a part of the magnificence that shimmered around them. Peggy whispered that every living thing had a radiance that lived forever, be it a memory, a child or love. Richard sighed when he thought of how she died in a car crash this time about a year ago.

Amy moved closer to him; her hands were warm. 'I'm sorry, Richard. I can't handle this isolation, this nothingness.' She slowly shook her head.

Richard tried to think of words to reassure her and share his sense of freedom on the open road, but nothing came. The pointers perched on a dead tree in front of them as they hurtled along the highway. Adelaide was still hundreds of miles away.

A distant single headlight suddenly appeared in the rear-view mirror. Richard glanced several times as it sped towards them. The bright light sat behind the boot. He was annoyed because whoever it was had their high beam on.

Amy gazed backwards. 'I can't hear any engine, Richard.'

'That's because he's behind us.'

'But normally with a motorbike whether it's in front of you or behind you, you hear something.'

'Not always. I've noticed that when you're out in the middle of nowhere, you don't hear anything until it passes you. How do you know it's a motorbike, eh?' Richard crinkled his eyes. The intense ball of light reminded him of the shooting star he'd seen earlier.

'I can't make out anything except for that single light.' She let go of his hand to twist around and notice that it didn't have the familiar look of a headlight. Its gold light constantly flared to light up their cabin like it was daylight.

The couple hurtled through the desert silence. A road sign told them that Bordertown was fifty miles away.

'Can't you speed up?' Amy leant towards him.

'I'm already pushing the old girl hard. Let me try something else first, OK darls?' He pressed down on the floor to click his high beam on. The highway in front of them was deserted. Richard put his blinker on to indicate that it was safe to pass. There was no response. He thought of how motorbikes normally leapt at the chance to overtake a car. The ball of light hung there like it had attached itself to the back of the car.

When Richard put his foot down on the accelerator, the light travelled at exactly the same speed. His speedometer needle made its way up to one hundred and twenty miles an hour. But it was no use; he failed to put any distance between himself and whatever it was behind them.

Richard lit another cigarette. The glare from whatever it was behind them hurt his tired eyes. Venus dangled below the crescent moon in the sky ahead. He knew their old bomb of a car wouldn't be able to keep it up for much longer.

Amy was speechless as they fled along the highway. The light trailed behind them like a ghost.

Richard eased up on the accelerator when they soared into a dip in the road. He saw the shadow of their car racing along in front of them.

Amy gasped as they flew up a rise. 'It's vanished!'

'God, maybe he's had an accident!' Richard touched the brakes.

'What are you doing?' Amy cried.

'Maybe it was a motorbike after all and the poor bugger's had an accident.' He pulled the car to the side of the road and flipped his indicator on.

'Richard, please doesn't!'

'There might be someone hurt back there, Amy.' Richard turned the car around. He leant over the steering wheel to peer through his high beam. He manoeuvred the car in circles around where they'd last seen the light. There were no skid marks or any other sign of a crash. It was as if it had disappeared straight into the rise on the road. Richard brought the car to a halt and opened his door.

'C'mon, let's get out of here!' Amy grabbed his arm.

Her large eyes made him hesitate. But he managed to stand up and take one last look around the black stillness, then got back in.

'Hoo-fucking-ray!' Richard shouted an hour later when they sped past the border sign. Amy chuckled after spotting some farm lights. They pulled in to the first motel. The ancient owner said they were lucky: she was just about to close. Amy noticed that the old lady had a gleam in her dark eye when Richard chatted to her about the strange light. She explained to the young couple that they had seen what the locals called a Min-Min light. They've been around since the Dreamtime; some people reckoned they were the spirits of the dead come back to guide the living.

Amy gave herself to their lovemaking that night. He smiled when he heard her talking in her sleep, then stepped out on to the veranda for a smoke. Richard thought of Peggy as he watched a falling star disappear into the embrace of the dunes. The night air embraced his naked flesh as he contemplated the mysteries of the desert.

Waiting For the Change

Julian crawled through the peak-hour traffic. The hazy skyline of the city sat in the rear-view mirror behind his bloodshot eyes. The surrounding paddocks were yellow and scarred by blotches of dead grass. Cows huddled under solitary trees, seeking strips of shade. The car temperature needle was stuck on hot.

His mind drifted back to previous summers. After three or four days of scorching weather, thunderstorms had always washed away the heat and dust. These days, if there was a change, the clouds didn't bring any rain and the mercury barely dropped. The news on the car radio said that the drought was now into its fourth month. Another forty-degree day was on its way. He gripped the steering wheel as the oven wind buffeted his car.

Julian's mind drifted back to when he had experienced his first drought as an eight-year-old boy. A dream he had back then entered into his tired mind. He was watering a dead garden, trying to bring withered plants back to life. White fleece-like clouds floated overhead. He pointed the hose at the clouds. They changed into a rust colour. The sky turned red as the clouds smashed into the ground with an almighty thud. He ran terrified towards his house through broken bits of cloud.

Melbourne had withered on the vine. Julian remembered the water restrictions and upturned beer bottles dug into yellow lawns. He recalled going to the drive-in with his folks when he couldn't see the movies due to ash falling down from a bushfire in the Dandenongs. Sleepless sweaty nights, the next day he'd been too exhausted to learn anything in primary school. Now here he was years later in the same blurred state, about to start teaching.

Once inside the corridors, Julian felt like a sacrificial lamb. He was overwhelmed by the adolescent hordes that were running, pushing, arguing and screaming around him. The teachers appeared friendly enough while they offered him reams of advice, but they didn't seem to listen to what he had to say.

He was directed to his cramped desk, given his chalk and pens, and sent on his way to the classroom. A knot squeezed his gut when he introduced himself to the class. The kids seemed sullen and ready to rebel.

Julian spent a long morning teaching them about the Eureka Stockade. He read aloud from the journal of Raffaelo Carboni. His curiosity was stirred when Carboni wrote that in the last days preceding the rebellion, the goldfields had been plagued by hot winds described as 'hurricane-like and horrible'. The teacher posed the question to his students; 'Do you think the rebellion would have occurred if the weather hadn't been so extreme?'

The kids remained silent; the heat had deflated their spirits down into a state of dreaming idleness. He remembered feeling exactly the same during that furnace summer when he was a boy. Mr Davidson, his bully of a teacher (how easily he recalled that hateful name), had strapped Julian if he wasn't paying attention. The razor-biting pain on his childish hand made no difference to his sluggish state of mind but it made him all the more determined to ignore Mr Arsehole Davidson's rantings.

Dominic knocked on Julian's caravan door in the afternoon, shouting, 'Hey, you lazy bugger, let's go down to the river.' As they walked towards the Yarra, Julian revealed his fears to his friend. He anxiously studied the white blue sky for any sign of a cool change while he spoke. A mustard sun slouched above the trees in a cloudless sky.

Dominic held his hand up to his friend. 'It's impossible to teach kids when they're conscripts. The sure way to turn kids off anything is to force then to do it. To me, it's bloody well obvious that you don't want to teach, so why don't you just chuck it in?'

'Maybe it's this crazy weather that's affecting me.' Julian scratched his fair beard. 'You know me: I always go slightly batty when there's a north wind. Besides, I want to make a difference. I just don't want any dreary nine-to-five job. God knows I've had enough boring jobs to last me a lifetime. I want to change this world a bit by teaching kids to think for themselves. We're surrounded by human blotting pads.'

'That's all well and good, but do you really think the kids will actually listen to what you have to say?'

Julian pondered his friend's question. Both of them sat down on a clay bank to watch the brown Yarra snake through the caravan park. Julian envied his friend's lifestyle. Dominic had been on the dole ever since Adam played fullback for Jerusalem. Dominic was an artist, spending most of his time composing strange landscapes that sprouted Christian and pagan symbols. When Dominic wasn't painting, he was reading. When he wasn't reading, he was discussing. Right now he was lecturing Julian loudly.

'Isn't it bloody obvious that your intuition is telling you not to teach? Look at all the signs. You're not sleeping, you look like you haven't eaten a decent meal for ages, you're miserable. You're a good poet: some of the stuff you've written over the years is great. I mean, you've written a lot of crap too, but occasionally you've written some little gems. You should stick to what you've got a talent for. Your heart's not really into teaching.'

Dominic's words buzzed around Julian's mind. He refused to accept his friend's argument, believing that it just wasn't that simple.

His stinging eyes spied a willy-willy over at the caravan park. It rattled like a train while it wreaked havoc. Dead gum leaves, branches, polystyrene cups, socks, undies, beer cans, feathers, chip packets, dunny paper all circled madly.

His black cat, Moogal, dived out of his caravan and trundled like a hippopotamus towards him. She rubbed his ankles with her dark head.

Julian crouched down and asked her, 'What do you think, my sweet puss? Should I teach or should I just throw it all away?'

Moogal wove around his legs purring and looked up to him as if to say, 'I don't give a shit what you do. Just feed me, fella.'

Nearby trees bowed towards the ground.

'God, listen to that bloody wind, will you.' Julian rubbed his eyes. 'You know, I met some farmers on my travels to New South Wales many moons ago. Do you know what they call these winds?'

'No. What?' Dominic wrinkled his forehead.

'Brickfielders.'

'Brickfielders. Why that?'

'As the desert breath blows over their farms, the wind bakes the soil into red and brown colours. Huge cracks appear until everywhere you look you're surrounded by what looks like fields of brick.'

'Blackfella winds.' Dominic shook his head.

'What?' Julian turned towards his friend.

'Blackfella winds. These winds are so alien to me. I sometimes think that they're sent form the ancestors of this country to remind us Europeans huddled on the coastal fringes that we don't understand or love this place yet.'

Red bands of twilight stretched over the sky. Julian narrowed his eyes. He felt as if his cheeks were on fire as he studied the bloated brow of the sun vanishing behind a nearby hill. 'It's like we're witnessing the death of a wrathful god.'

Julian lit a cigarette and lay back on the grass. He heard a hissing sound. He wasn't sure if it was the rapids nearby or the sound of his own blood flowing through his tired brown veins. Moogal rustled overhead in the branches like a restless monkey.

A fortnight passed, a fortnight of seething winds, headaches and sleepless nights.

One afternoon, Julian observed giant heads of red-brown smoke marching across the caravan park. The sun was eclipsed by a swirling red wall of dust. At night he heard the wail of fire engines. He listened to radio reports of what they began to call Ash Wednesday. The next day as he taught, the knot in his stomach tightened. He dragged his feet around the classroom and murmured to the kids.

The north wind dragged Julian out of his sleep. His caravan swayed like a ship out at sea. Outside, he could hear an old gum tree sway and groan as its huge trunk fought the hot wind. A limb fell on the caravan roof. He sat up cursing and pulled back the blind to see a crescent moon plough through orange-coloured clouds.

Moogal leapt through the window. The moon reflected in her lizard green eyes when she pounced upon his bed. Her long black tail flicked. Her ears stretched backwards, her eyes bulged wildly.

'I know how you feel,' whispered Julian, while he scratched the base of her spine and stroked the length of her tail. He slumped back and dozed as Moogal purred and fell asleep on his pillow.

The knot in his stomach gradually dissolved with every mile that he travelled away from the school. His clothes sat next to him, stuffed into a green rubbish bag. His books were carefully slotted into every nook and cranny of the car. Moogal was asleep in her favourite cardboard fruit box in the back seat.

He'd rung Dominic and told him he was sick and tired of waiting for the change. He had no idea where he was going, just south, towards the ocean and away from the dust-caked city.

The Shoreline

A white beam cut through the night sky like a searchlight. It was coming up from the south, across the ocean. The beam was still and constant. Suddenly two other trails of light appeared on either side of the original. Three beams of pure white were piercing the night sky. On the horizon the ocean rippled within a ghostly white glow. More beams appeared in the sky, exactly like the original. Rowan counted twelve; he was transfixed by this unearthly display.

His limbs turned luminous, mirroring the light of the southern sky. Insects that had previously been droning through the bush were now silent. The ocean appeared still. Rowan could just hear a calm tide somewhere below the track he was standing on.

The cathedral of lights were turning to a rust colour. The same shade he'd observed on some of the foreshore rocks that jutted out of the ocean as the tide receded. The surrounding tea trees were bathed in an intense ochre. Slowly, the dozen ochre beams transformed. They started to ripple and shimmer, and began to melt into each other, until they looked like some vast velvet curtain, hovering over a purple ocean.

Rowan realised that he was witnessing the auroran lights. He'd heard the locals saying that you could see them once in a blue moon down here at Cape Otway. His mind marvelled at the thought that these southern lights snaked for thousands of miles all the way from Antarctica.

Rowan ran back along the track. He had to show Basia this magical sight before it disappeared. He staggered into the doorway of their cabin. No lights were on; a faint red glow flickered from the lounge room hearth. Rowan quietly walked into the bedroom. Basia was asleep.

Basia had been complaining of a bad headache, probably from the long drive along the Great Ocean Road. It took them about three hours to get to Cape Otway from Melbourne. She had nibbled like a squirrel at the meal Rowan had prepared for her, became tired, silent, and went to lie down. Rowan built a fire for her, then went off for a walk.

She was lying on her side. The ochre light was trickling through the cabin window; it seemed to sparkle on her dark brown hair. Her pale Polish face and exposed arms were cocooned in auroran light. The blankets hugged the curve of her hip. Rowan decided not to waken her. He reluctantly turned away from her to go outside.

He sat on the nearest log and proceeded to roll a cigarette. It was one of his favourite pastimes to smoke outside and study the night sky. He loved the way the smoke curled through his lungs and made his blood flow quicker. The light were dissolving now, falling back into the original single beam, which then transformed into a faint silver-blue cloud. The cloud hovered then slowly sailed towards the horizon. Waves of tiredness gradually overtook Rowan. He shuffled back inside, peeled off his clothes, then slowly curled into the back of Basia's still body. She half stirred to grasp his hugging left arm, sighed, then fell back into her slumber.

Through the corner of his drooping left eye he saw the dying remnant of the auroran light. The silver-blue wisp dropped into the horizon of the now black sea; it seemed to sizzle as it disappeared. The lapping of the tide gently stilled Rowan, then took him away somewhere to dream, while a sea mist enclosed their cabin.

Rowan woke up next morning to observe a nearby tentacle of mist slowly hoist its way from the shoreline to rest on a nearby hill. It glistened in the sun like a phosphorescent white snake. Rowan loved this coastline. He'd been coming down here off and on for years. One of his first memories was as a three-year-old being overwhelmed by the sight of the monolithic Apostles looming out of the ocean. He also vaguely recalled that on the same trip he was distressed at the sight of his ill mother needing to lie down early at night. His older sister said he cried all night. It was only a few years ago that Rowan discovered that his mother wasn't ill at all, but heavily drunk. She and her Irish father had stopped at practically every pub on the Great Ocean Road. Rowan chuckled to himself.

His quiet laughter roused Basia. He gently stroked her cheekbone and closed eyelids. He whispered, 'How are you, sweetie?'

'A lot better,' came her hushed reply. She cuddled into Rowan as he told her of the auroran lights. She stroked his skinny stomach as he imparted his story like an excited little boy. She loved his sense of wonder at things.

During the afternoon, the autumn sun started to break through the sea mist. Rowan decided to go for a swim. Basia was terrified by the idea; she'd never swum in a surf beach before. She decided to stay behind; besides she didn't bring any bathers.

'Bathers!' Rowan blurted out in amazement. 'You don't need bathers. Just swim in the nuddie like I do.'

Basia reeled at this suggestion. She replied, 'I'd prefer to stay behind, if you don't mind, Rowan. I'm still rather tired after our drive. I'd like to sit and read.'

'No worries, Basia,' Rowan responded, putting on a cheerful exterior.

She watched Rowan march down the track towards the beach, till his red hair and red beard disappeared into the tea trees. She slowly looked about her to realise the cabin was perched on the edge of the huge Otway forest. She felt the wilderness sit heavy upon the back of her neck. She turned back inside to try and lose herself in her book.

Rowan had thrown himself into the surging ocean to bodysurf. He loved the way the waves would pick up his body to carry him like the hand of God all the way back to the shoreline. He loved the smell and taste of the ocean always feeling reborn after a good swim. Rowan wished Basia could share his love of the open sea; his feelings of disappointment in her were gradually washed away by the battling waves.

At dusk they decided to get into the car and find the nearest lookout, in case the auroran lights returned. The sun was setting like a jaundiced spider through crimson and yellow clouds. Cold winds buffered the car. The occasional kestrel hovered over the shore, anxious for prey. Rowan placed his arm around Basia, she leant into him. She seemed preoccupied.

'What is it, Basia?' Rowan asked.

'Oh nothing. I was just thinking of something that happened to me in the past,' Basia said.

'And what was that?'

'This sunset reminds me of when I was a teenager with my father.'

'Yeah and…?' Rowan said.

'I was only thirteen. I'd just menstruated for the first time. I was horrified. My mother told my father. He made me sit in the kitchen to listen to him. The sun was setting just as it is now. My dad said to me through the shadows of dusk that I was a woman now. I had to be responsible. All I could see was his silhouette. Eeverything around us was red, the sunset made the kitchen seem like it was on fire. My dad loomed over me like Jehovah. I was terrified!'

Dark blue clouds sat on the horizon like a large vaporous mountain range. The first shade of night started to undermine the dusk. Rowan pondered over Basia's parents, Wojtek and Marila. Old Wojtek didn't strike him as the Jehovah type. Whenever Rowan would visit, Wojtek was always chatty, plying the younger man with mountains of Polish food and endless glasses of wine. They'd often sit out on the veranda, smoking cartons of cigarettes, discussing history and politics. Marila would be out there too, illuminated by the wine and good conversation. Basia would sit inside reading giving Rowan a curious stare each time he'd come inside.

Wojtek and Marila had both been through the war. Wojtek's speech would always slow down when he'd recall the bombing of Warsaw and how he was taken from Poland and forced to work on a German farm as a labourer. Marila had an academic career in literature cut short, when the Germans forced her to work in a munitions factory. Both were treated as slaves, yet neither of them hated the Germans. Rowan was amazed.

At times, Marila appeared desperate to be heard; a disturbed, lost gleam came over her eyes as she struggled to find words that were always inadequate to express how she really felt. Basia had inherited that strange look from her mother. Rowan remembered the first time he'd seen the look was in the office cafeteria. Rowan just begun temporary work in the Department of Immigration. Basia had been with the department for sixteen years. She was sitting by herself when Rowan cautiously approached her. Somehow they stumbled into conversation about travel. Rowan was planning a trip to Ireland. Basia quietly mentioned that she'd been back to Poland twice.

Basia found that, despite her best efforts, she opened up to Rowan. Perhaps it was the way his youthful blue eyes would light up in amazement or the way he'd toy with ideas, never accepting anything on face value. She found his childlike wonder refreshing.

Then came that curious look over her face when she started to talk of her journey to Auschwitz. Rowan wanted to hug her on the spot; he didn't know why. Maybe it was, of all things, the conversation about the death camp.

'Death, ugly bile-dripping death,' Rowan recalled, shouting to himself inside. 'I've just lost my grandfather, whom I worshipped. I feel so fucking well lost.' Now here he was almost two years later on, sitting in the darkness with her, perched on a cliff stroking her brow, watching the vast indifferent waters of Bass Strait.

The shrill of a plover stirred him from his thoughts. He looked over at Basia; she was silent, enjoying his gentle strokes. He took his arms away to roll a cigarette. Basia watched his Celtic face flare in the darkness as he lit his match.

He muttered, 'It looks like no auroran lights tonight.'

The clouds of twilight had dissolved into the night; giant walls of sea mist were now silently forming out at sea. Pretty soon the pale walls would start to march towards the shoreline.

Rowan lit a fire when they got back to their cabin and produced a bottle of red wine. He sat near the flames and loved the way the combination of an open fire, and red wine, would make his body glow in sensuous delight. His eyes reflected the expanding yellow flames and his mind danced with the sound of the ocean wind fanning the hearth.

Basia was sitting away from Rowan in the darkness, sipping her wine, observing his abandon. She cautiously asked across the room, 'Don't you ever feel the difference in our age, Rowan?'

Summoned from his daydreaming, Rowan took a long time to reply, 'No way, Basia. I never sense any age barrier, do you?'

Basia was eight years older than Rowan; she felt it all the time. Anxious not to hurt him, she stated, 'Yes, I do sometimes. You take obvious delight in things, like when we go for a walk, you'll suddenly stop to watch and listen to a particular bird, or take in a view. I'd naturally miss all that if I was by myself, because I'm so old.'

Over the past two years, Rowan had continuously heard these claims of old age on Basia's part. 'Listen to you – "so old",' he replied. 'My God, you're only thirty-four, Basia.' Out of frustration, he added, 'You're sounding like an old grandmother.'

'I am an old grandmother,' she cried back.

'In that case, Granny, come and sit on your grandson's knee, because he's feeling frisky towards his old grandma tonight.'

'Oh, Rowan,' she laughingly complained. Basia slowly walked across to the hearth and placed herself upon his lap. She felt the warmth of the fire upon her back as she responded to his kisses. His lips tasted of salt and wine.

Who is this man? she asked herself internally. This crazy man who keeps diving in and out of the sea naked, like some demented merman, who has no respect for any belief, who once called my Christian religion a lovely myth.

Rowan sensed Basia was churning something over in her mind. Much as he enjoyed this moment with her, he wished that just for once she would let her mind rest, her body relax.

'What is it, Basia?' he whispered while kissing her eyelids. 'You seem to be out of sorts.'

'I don't know,' she said. The constant lapping of the tide almost made her feel dizzy and sickly. When she had stepped out into the hazy light of the afternoon, she felt as if something has slithered from the forest shadows to possess her.

'There must be something that coloured your mood. Is it me?' he asked.

'No. I don't know!' she almost pleaded.

Rowan backed off and poured himself another glass of wine.

It's not you, Basia thought to herself. It's me. I just can't share your joy of life. There's so much I want to tell you but I just don't think you'd understand. You're a free spirit constantly up in the clouds. Me, I'm manacled to the ground. But who knows, I truly don't know why I'm depressed.

They both sat silent, watching the red coal of the fire ebb and crumble into the hearth.

Later what night, Rowan went for a walk, brooding over Basia. He had pictured himself and Basia walking together on the beach at night. Instead, here he was alone, peering through patches of sea mist at the night sky. He spied his old companion, Sirius the Dog Star, leaving a blue trail of starlight over the black ocean. Is it ever possible to truly know another person on this planet? he asked himself. Maddened seagulls fled along the swirling blue trail of starlight. Rowan wondered whether birds navigated by Sirius at night.

He sat on a log to observe another break in the mist; long white weaving corridors of mist revealed a bloated king tide. Rowan watched as a vast dark wall formed on the horizon; the walls grew and seemed to travel forever towards the shoreline. Suddenly they developed pale foaming heads and roared as they smashed onto the beach in front of him. The backbone of the waves continuously curled, twisted and sped like giant snakes.

He remembered on that trip with his grandfather how he was

terrified by the ocean. His grandfather sat him on his lap held his tiny cold hand and sang cooing sounds into his ear. The old man's voice eased him. Suddenly, a mutton bird landed near Rowan. Too tired to move, it just sat there. Together they took in the surging ocean.

Basia heard the distant drone of the car engine as she hovered on the borderline between sleep and wakefulness. Rowan felt claustrophobic as the suburbs started crowding in around him. Her spirits lifted when she finally saw the grey, square landscape of the city. She suddenly became talkative and happy. Rowan, puzzled by her transformation, half responded to her small talk.

The Milk Run

I'd just discovered something unfortunate about Stephen at our going-away do. He's been to a hypnotherapist and has given up the fags. As I got stuck into a bottle of red and danced to Jimmy Hendrix, Stephen crouched on the floor telling our friend Sophie all about his struggle. She sat next to him with a look of admiration then gave me the occasional serious stare with those piercing brown eyes of hers as I gyrated with a fag dangling out of my lips.

Ah well! I suppose now's as good as time as any to give up. I can see it from Stephen's point of view. He probably figures now that we're about to embark on the big trip to Europe, it's best to start with a clean slate. I can respect his way of thinking. He's right, seeing that there's no guarantee we'll ever come back; Stephen's marriage has dissolved and I'm bored shitless living in this country. Why not start a fresh new chapter in our lives by giving up a vice? Besides, there was that look he kept getting from Sophie.

I puff on my last three cigarettes the morning we're due to take off. God I love sitting outside; it's been my ritual for yonks. Blowing smoke up into a different Melbourne sky every morning. Cigarettes and a cup of coffee for breakfast. Ah! It's the perfect excuse for getting away from it all. Sophie once told me that I would still go outside and study the sky even if I didn't smoke. Maybe she's right. I stub my last cigarette into the ground and chuck my empty packet into the rubbish bin.

Stephen and I look at each other and roar with laughter as our jumbo soars off the tarmac. The outer suburbs vanish below us and pretty soon we're flying over the bush. I'm zooming off to fulfil a long-held dream to return to my ancestral home, Ireland.

My granddad Alan raised me to see myself as an Irish-Australian. He hardly talked about the big feller upstairs, preferring instead to share with me his belief in Mother Nature and the simple things in life. Trouble was, this outlook didn't really fit in with a nation of greed merchants. So here I am, Alan, flying back to our tribe and having a drink for you, old son. God, this beer's going down well. I'd love a cigarette right now but decide against it.

We fly over the highlands where our family settled a hundred years ago. They took a selection along the King River and ran some cattle and sheep. I always feel at home when I go up to north-east Victoria; it's Kelly country. The bush is full of ghosts; if you wander deep into the forests up there you can feel old Ned's presence. His angry spirit still roams the countryside demanding justice for his family.

After a few generations, our family started growing tobacco, that lovely brown weed that weaves through your lungs. Maybe if I have another beer it'll kill the urge. Thank God we booked in the non-smoking section of the plane, although you can still smell the ciggies up here.

The booking! Stephen and I couldn't believe our luck. It only cost us $750 one way to London. $750! What a bargain flying Singapore Airlines and Air Pakistan. After getting our tickets, we went straight to a pizza parlour in Lygon Street and celebrated. Stephen and I ordered the biggest pizza you could buy and a bottle of red vino. How we ate, laughed, drank and smoked!

Stephen doesn't laugh as much as he used to; it must be the withdrawals. He reckons it's like wrestling with a monster that wants to sink its clutches into your body. Apart from feeling a bit light-headed, I don't feel too bad. Oh well, maybe some fresh air and exercise in Ireland will do us both the world of good. Time for another drink.

The captain says we're going to land in Brisbane, which is a bit of a surprise, because I thought we were flying to Singapore. The light up here is so glaring and harsh. Look at all those tropical plants; you wouldn't credit we were on the same continent. We wait on the tarmac for a couple of hours in the heat while everyone finds their seats and shoves their luggage in. Phew! It's so hot and muggy, not like the dry heat you get in Melbourne. I wonder if I should mosey on down to the smokers and bot a cigarette? Nah. Sophie wouldn't be too impressed.

We're off again, thank God! You really get an idea of the vastness of the place we live in. The jumbo's engines hum; we're flying hundreds of miles an hour but it feels like we're stuck over the desert. Jesus, look at that ancient worn landscape, everything's so red! It takes over five hours just to get out of Australia.

Indonesia: everything looks lush, the colours are so different, the huge clouds we glide over are silver-blue. I remember those crap Indonesian cigarettes I use to puff at university. They were herbal and didn't have any nicotine in them. You could still indulge in the sensation of smoking but it wasn't addictive. Didn't work for me, though. It was like sucking a dry cabbage; my mouth used to feel like the bottom of a cockie's cage. I soon went back to the Peter Jacksons. I remember the way I used to chain-smoke all night when I was writing an essay. They were the good old days when you could smoke in a lecture or tutorial.

Singapore: their huge bloody terminal makes Tullamarine look like a country airport. It's like a giant shopping centre here. Stephen and I disembark and wait for our connecting flight to Karachi. Everyone in the lounge is having a fag. I wonder if they sell those crap cigarettes here? Here comes a waitress; I order a beer. She comes back with a can and tells me it's $5. Five bloody dollars: what a rip-off! I grumpily pay. We try to relax in the humidity.

The Air Pakistan jumbo has got all these broken air conditioning switches and the oxygen's vents hiss over some of the seats; the cabin roof's covered in condensation. I look at Stephen and ask him if he's sure about this. He reckons we don't have any choice and a least we're on the road to Karachi. I shrug and sit down. Ah, at last! We roar straight up into the sky but zoom back down again to land in Kuala Lumpur then wait another hour for people to board the plane. Jesus Harry Percival! It was like the roller coaster ride at Luna Park.

We fly to Bangkok and sit on the tarmac to wait another fucking hour for people to get on the plane. This isn't a bloody flight, it's a milk run! The nicotine monster is starting to possess me, my lungs gasp for a cigarette! I can't even drink because this useless bloody airline doesn't serve alcohol.

The captain tells us it will take approximately eight hours to fly to Karachi. When the plane takes off, I decide to try and have a snooze. My decision is reinforced when an Eddie Murphy movie comes on. After a long struggle I find myself drifting off. Ah! Ripples of sleep drift over my body! Ah! What the fuck's that? Something's stabbing me in the side; my dozing body's leaning over the aisle. I open my eyes.

The steward is poking me. 'You have drink!' He's holding up a tray full of boring orange juice.

'I don't want a drink!' I'm no good when someone wakes me up.

'You have drink!'

'I don't want a bloody drink!' I'm really pissed off now because once I'm awake I'll stay awake.

In fact, I'm fully conscious all the way to Karachi. I feel like slapping Stephen when I see his big round head nodding off. Maybe now's my chance to sneak off down the back of the plane and bot a cigarette. Nah, he'll smell me. Well, if he can give up, then so can I! I'll be able to write to Sophie and tell her I've kicked the habit too.

Stephen and I finally arrive at Karachi in the wee hours of the morning. We're told to disembark again while they refuel and clean out the plane. As the bus takes us to the terminal, I'm struck by the desert dryness; it reminds me of home. I look up to see a crescent moon dangling below Venus. The airport is full of Pakistani soldiers wielding machine guns.

I've only been journeying for twenty-four hours, but I'm already getting a sense of this huge world we inhabit and how Australia is only a tiny part of it. I stare back at the sky to realise that night has vanished: the moon, Venus, the stars, they've disappeared! It's like someone has flicked a switch. I guess the tropics don't have dusk!

Stephen and I excitedly chat in the airport lounge. Despite my nicotine craving and tiredness, I find this place exotic. There are thousands of people bustling around here; there's not a suit or tie in sight. Clothes are worn to highlight spirituality rather than commerce. It makes a nice change.

Nobody pays any attention to the stewards as they go through the safety drill before we take off. Everyone's gas-bagging; people have their bare feet resting on the back of the seats in front of them. We zoom off once more and I start yarning with the Pakistani bloke sitting next to me. We talk cricket, we speculate on how the test match has barely altered since medieval times. I tell him I love the way the game is subject to the vagaries of the weather and how two teams can battle for five days and still not get a result. He says cricket is like a religion in Pakistan. His people revere Bradman as a god and if he'd been born in the subcontinent there would be a temple devoted to him. He tells me that the Waugh brothers have so such potential and it won't be long before Australia becomes a world power. That'd make a nice change!

Our plane banks over Istanbul; I don't believe it when I actually see the huge dome and minarets of St Sophia. Look at that thing, I nudge Stephen and point, it was built over fourteen hundred years ago by the Emperor Justinian. Byzantium was such a mysterious empire. We were taught that Rome fell in the fourth century. Yet it wasn't so. The ancient world lived on for a further thousand years. As we walk around the airport, Stephen tells me Gallipoli is just down the road. I realise that I will be the first in the family to return to Europe peacefully; my uncles fought in both world wars.

We stick our heads out of the jumbo at Amsterdam to experience European light for the first time. It's pale and soft; colours are subdued here. I find that I don't have to squint like I normally do back home. Stephen and I have been flying for a day and a half now.

Our jumbo is suddenly enveloped by a huge cloud bank over the English Channel. How on earth do they manage to navigate through this stuff?

We touch down at Heathrow. There is an endless line of jets waiting to take off. Stephen and I shuffle off with our Pakistani friends, who are a lot warmer than the English customer fossils we have to deal with. We book our flight to Dublin then wait another three hours. I reach the stage where I can hardly think any more.

Ireland! Our Aer Lingus jets breaks through the clouds as we view the patchwork emerald green fields for the first time, I get shivers up and down my spine! We've finally made it after forty-two hours.

Dublin airport's so tiny. The lady at the counter says in a beautiful accent that she feels sorry for our tired look, then books in a bed and breakfast for us in Drumchondra.

Stephen throws his pack on the floor and falls into bed. I look out the window to notice the Brian Boru Hotel across the road. Stephen snores; I hear the patter of rain on the roof.

Beautiful Dublin rain lulls me off to sleep. For the first time in two days, I know exactly where I'm going after we wake up and what I'm going to do.

Give it a Whirl

So far, so good. The roads around this part of Ireland are perfectly flat or downhill. Stephen and I hired a couple of bikes back in Wicklow and are making our way to Glendalough. After flying down a weaving road and getting our bearings over a stone bridge, we decide to have morning tea at Rathdrum.

I love the way the locals pronounce the name of this tiny town 'Ruttrum'. When we ask for directions, 'Ruttrum's hill down' so many miles. We're told to be careful about the Devil's Glen on our way back. Just exactly what the Devil's Glen is, I'm not sure. Maybe these people think we're Yankee tourists and are having a lend of us.

As we slurp our tea, I realise that I haven't been on a bike for over a decade. My last ride was when Stephen and I were teenagers. We used to love cycling out into the bush. Until today, I'd forgotten all about the freedom of pedalling along an open road and of being miles away from the noisy madness of the suburbs.

That's one thing I've loved about my mate; he's always open to the idea of getting away from it all. When we were twenty, we quit our dead-end jobs and hitch-hiked around Tasmania to then end up on a hippie farm.

Stephen gets up from the table and studies the overcast sky; the clouds are high so we should be right.

The road gets smaller once we're out of town; it's more like a lane and we're starting to go uphill. But we don't mind because we've just entered into our first European forest. The trees are so thick and lush; they bulge over the road. It's so silent here; the only thing you can hear is the whir of our wheels and crackle of our tyres on the road. Stephen says it's like we've stepped into something out of King Arthur. Huge elm, oak, beech, pine and ash trees blot out the sky; our tiny road is bordered by endless hedgerows. As we cycle through this shadow land, the occasional jackdaw croaks on a high branch somewhere. When we first came across these birds at the ancient capital of Tara, Stephen said they were guardians of the old ways.

It's starting to drizzle but, being Melbourne boys, we're prepared with beanies and raincoats. Our tyres hiss as we weave through the Wicklow Mountains. Droplets of rain plop on my hood; my panting breath turns to mist. I turn around to see Stephen. With the huge blue raincoat his mum has bought him, he looks like a monk. I stand upon the pedals and flex every muscle in my body. There's not another soul on the road. Any minute now, I expect to see a cloaked Druid making his way through the shades with his oak staff.

We come to the tiny village of Laragh around midday. Stephen and I get a spring in our heel when we spot a pub. We order a pot of tea each and toasted sandwiches, then stand beside the open fire to thaw our limbs. The publican tells us that Glendalough is just down the road. We gobble down our sandwiches, polish off our tea then order another pot while waiting for the rain to clear. As we lounge around, I notice how we've both developed a healthy gold sheen to our skin.

The first thing I see when back on the road is a giant dark green mountain with a sheer wall plunging down into a valley. Large trees dot the spine of the mountain; they look like a long column of cavalry. I spot a graveyard up ahead full of Celtic crosses and leaning tombstones. A round tower suddenly looms out of the landscape together with the ruins of a several medieval churches. Stephen and I get off our bikes to investigate.

We learn that St Kevin lived in this area in the sixth century. He came from the royal house of Leinster and as a boy, while being tutored by three holy men, came to Glendalough to live inside a tree. I look at the misty wilderness surrounding me and imagine a fair-haired boy cautiously poking his head out of a crack in a trunk. Kevin left but later returned to spend his days as a hermit in a cave. When news spread that a holy man lived in this neck of the woods, his isolation came to an end. We walk towards his tiny stone church behind the graveyard. Unlike the others, it's still intact. It's about the size of a small house with a steep stone roof and a round tower-like belfry. A nearby forest stretches up a hill.

The combination of natural and man-made beauty strikes me. Back home, buildings in a wilderness area are merely functional. I love the idea that this simple structure was dedicated to a man who strove for communion with his maker through nature's silence. Stephen tells me St Kevin's steep roof reminds him of the shape of the mountains around us. We chat about being surprised by the humility of this little church; the way it was designed to blend in rather than dominate the landscape. In Melbourne, our churches always seem to scramble for the most prominent location.

Stephen and I explore the round tower before getting back onto our bikes. It was built as a lookout and defence against the Vikings and had a door high up into which a ladder could be pulled once everyone was safe inside. It saddens me to think those bastards made it all the way up here to sack the place. Stephen reckons Vikings were the yobbos of the Middle Age.

As we cycle further down into the valley, a brown lake appears on our left-hand side. My cheeks and fingers sting in the cold air. The surrounding mountains are thickly carpeted in forest. Clouds of mist slowly drift over the water. The sky looks threatening but we've been lucky since we left the pub. The lake expands as we glide down the road. We weave around the final bend to be greeted by a magical view. A vast brown body of water overshadowed by the steep shoulders of three dark mountains. I follow Stephen's pointing arm to the other side of the lake to make out a silver waterfall below a strand of mist. Grey sky and shadowed mountains reflect in the calm waters of Glendalough.

Stephen and I park our bikes then take a few swigs of water. He starts cracking jokes about the place being 'picturesquesky'. It was a word we made up down in Tasmania. Whenever we came across a beautiful view, we'd say it was 'picturesquesky', which means it's a great place to pitch your esky. My mate and I cack ourselves silly then decide to head for the waterfall.

We see an ancient stone cross and stone circle. The green tourist plaque tells us they're the remains of an early Christian fort. Stephen and I walk along the edge of the lake and discover a pine forest. I look above the trees to notice the crest of the mountain is rust-brown and completely exposed. Stephen start pretending he's Merlin and tells me he can see into the future. I ask him that if this is so, then why did he decide to barrack for such a crap team as St Kilda? He replies that adversity is character-forming.

I hear a strange voice in the distance. We stop to listen. Stephen squints as we slowly make out the sound of a woman's voice singing. Merlin turns to me and says, 'It's the Lady of the Lake come to bequeath Excalibur.' I nervously laugh when he tells me to be on the lookout for a woman's arm extending out of the water with a sword in her hand.

We step out of the forest into a land of brown heath strewn with grey boulders. As I start to hear the hiss of the waterfall, the woman's voice becomes louder. Well, she ain't no woodland sprite; she's a chubby little woman with a mop of blonde curly hair. Without any prompting, she proceeds to tell us her name, her town and which state she comes from in America. We learn that she wants to be an opera singer and loves practising outside.

I sit down on a rock and attempt to take in the view of Glendalough while she small talks to Stephen. I marvel at the way this valley was carved out by a glacier during the Ice Age. It's like a giant has hacked away with his chisel at the side of the mountains and left his trailings scattered around this side of the lake. The water darkens and I look up to see a black peninsula of cloud heading our way.

The afternoon's getting on and I suggest that it's time to make tracks. Stephen and Madame Butterball agree. It rains as we head back through the pine forest. I pull my beanie down over my ears and button up my raincoat while Madame Butterball caterwauls away. My legs start to hurt as I think of various tortures I could subject her to.

We mercifully part ways at the car park then Stephen and I take shelter to consult our map. He tells me he's totally rooted. I respond likewise and we agree to head home for Wicklow before it gets dark. We single out a road that looks shorter and more direct than the one we used earlier on, then console ourselves that it'll probably be hill down for most of the way.

As Stephen and I struggle uphill on our bikes past St Kevin's, I make a vow to return to this place before we leave Ireland. I turn around to take one last view of the valley and make out the silhouette of the round tower against the dimming sky.

We cruise past the inviting lights of the pub in Laragh. The roads are downhill and straight. I look up into the twilight sky and decide to let her rip. I pedal furiously for a wee bit and then fly down the mountain road. Whee! I'm approaching warp speed! Stephen rapidly disappears behind me. Zoom! Another tiny village flies past and I notice that all the sensible people are inside out of the bucketing rain.

It's getting dark on the road but at least there are no cars about. The spray from the road leaks into my feet. I feel this bone-aching weariness slowly spread from my legs to the rest of my body. I'm thankful that I don't have to pedal now and only have to cling to the handlebar for dear life. I wonder how my mate's getting on?

There's a sign up ahead. The Devil's Glen! So it's a real place! Now why the bloody hell do I have to be careful around here? OK, the road's dipping. Jesus Harry, it's really steep! Hmm…there are some hairy corners around here; that last one was a doozy. The wheels creak while I try to struggle to slow down. It suddenly becomes jet-black. I look around me to realise that I'm in the middle of a heavily wooded forest! I take my frozen hand off the brake.

All the shops in the small town of Ashford are closed. I chuck a right and when I when I come over a hill I see the lights of Wicklow! I pedal like a lunatic for a short spurt and then scream down the lovely straight stretch of road before me. Zoom goes another village!

It rains cats and dogs as I'm transformed into a speeding cloud of drizzle. Water pours off my forehead and drips off my nose. I can hardly see. I'm beyond care by the time I reach the outskirts of the town. I thread through the light traffic to behold the wondrous sight of our double-storey bed and breakfast. I park my bike out the back and stagger upstairs for a shower.

I feel like an iceberg but the warm water slowly restores feeling to my body. I drape my dripping clothes over the oil heater then fall onto my bed and stare out through the moisture on my window at the glistening street lights.

I doze off for a bit, then hear Stephen ringing his bike bell to announce he's made it home. He sticks his round face through the doorway and stares at me. I see that my friend's face is devoid of any spark of life; his saggy features remind me of a bloodhound.

'Do I look as shithouse as you do?' Stephen asks with a groan.

'Yes!' I feebly reply as the poor bugger shuffles off like a Frankenstein monster to the shower.

He showers long, close to an hour, in fact, then collapses on to his bed. Stephen and I moan to each other. We're both ravenous but are too exhausted to do anything about it.

Austin, the owner of the bed and breakfast, sticks his bespectacled head around our door. 'Are you fellas all right there?'

'We've just got back from Glendalough. We're knackered.' I feel like a tortoise stuck on his back as I try to lean up.

'That's grand. Do you Aussies feel like some *craic* tonight? I've organised a set dance down at the local hall.'

'Umm…no thanks, we've had a big day and decided to stay in for the night, thanks for asking, Austin,' Stephen gasps while he rubs his legs.

'There'll be lots of local lasses coming. We need a few fellas to make up the numbers. We're off to the Grand Hotel afterwards.' Austin raises his silver eyebrows.

Stephen and I pause to think for a second.

'I suppose we could give it a whirl. What do you reckon?' I finally manage to get myself upright.

'A short and merry life,' Stephen chuckles as he hauls his weary bones up.

Austin gets up on the stage and explains the moves to everyone in between songs. I never knew dancing could be so complicated and have discovered that traditional Irish songs can go on forever. To get the set dancing right, you have to move every fibre in your ankle and legs. The lower half of my body feels like it's been immersed in the flames of hell. The fiddles and accordion start up once more and I stare across the dance floor to notice that Stephen has a look of sheer agony on his face.

After a few pints at the Grand later on, and in the company of some rather spunky Irish women, we manage to overcome our pain.

The Golden Glasses

'See dat house top of da hill, Aussie?' An old fella standing out the front of the pub pointed to a dimly lit house perched on a nearby rocky outcrop.

Squadrons of humming insects circled the pub's outdoor light.

'Yeah, I do.' I couldn't see much just the outline of an old house, with faint silver light trickling out of the windows.

'Well, I wouldn't be goin' anywhere near dere if oi was you,' he said with a frightened rabbit look on his face.

'How come?' I crinkled my face and took another drag on my cigarette. I almost lost my breath as the Atlantic wind whipped the smoke away.

'Oid rather not say, Aussie.' The old man slowly shook his head.

'What is it?' This guy's serious, I thought to myself.

'Oid rather not say.'

I'd just farewelled my drinking mate Johnny after he'd zigzagged off towards direction of the forbidden house. After quite a few pints of Guinness, we got to that leaning over and talking to each other face to face stage. I met Johnny after witnessing the most spectacular sunset I'd ever seen in my life. This part of Ireland's completely different to the rest. The Burren's a limestone wilderness where there's not a tree in sight. It's like a giant's come along and dragged his club along the coastline to leave nothing but rubble in his wake.

Stephen and I threw our backpacks into the deserted youth hostel then sat outside for a cup of tea. A jackdaw nested on the roof. The sun turned molten it as hovered over the Atlantic. It then bloated up like a nuclear bomb. When it plunged into the water, I expected a hiss. The sun's rays reflected off the limestone mountains surrounding us, and before we knew it, Stephen and I were bathed in intense solar light. My mate transformed into the Cheshire cat; all I could see was his smiling teeth. His form together with any other form all merged into this blinding red sea of light. All of a sudden, the lighthouse from Aran Isle just across the water swept through the dusk. Stephen saw I was ecstatic. He got the turf fire going and starting making our tea. I had to write.

> Sunset at Fanore
>
> Fierce gold red sun
> melts over the isles,
> simmering old head lunges,
> dragging flared canopies behind,
> violet fingers of cloud
> darken, crimson mists
> gather to shroud
> the outstretched solar limbs,
> blood red flames hang over my brow
> flagstones catch fire,
> vast blue blinding patches hover
> over this rippling vision of time.
> Lighthouse of Aran hurls his flame
> rhythmic beams flare my study white,
> flickering hearth shadows bounce on the pane,
> tides bear me through this long writing night.

The sun kindled inside of my gut; my poem was finished, I needed another outlet, so I went to the local pub. It was full of old skinny fellas, all dressed in faded worn suits and caps, who spoke Gaelic. Johnny appeared out of nowhere after I ordered my first pint of Guinness. He stuck out from the rest of the patrons; for starters, he was young and animated. All the old fellas seemed to whisper like old oak trees and stood as rigid as the capstones around me. They had brown weather-beaten faces, whereas Johnny's was pink and fresh. He wore a colourful purple shirt with a blue vest covered in moons and stars, whereas the old fellas favoured grey or beige. He spoke no Gaelic.

'So what brings ya to dis God-forsaken country, Aussie?' Johnny's luminous blue eyes twinkled at me.

'How did you know I was an Aussie?'

'Ah, tis your accent. It sticks out loike a pair of dog's balls when I heard you order. Johnny's the name.'

'You're not wrong,' I tittered back to him. 'I can't get over your lovely lyrical accents, whereas we Aussies all sound like constipated crows. Mike's mine.'

Johnny belly laughed as he shook my hand. I stroked the red stubble of my beard and explained to him that my recently deceased grandfather told us that his father came from County Clare. I was here to fulfil my grandfather's dream of returning to Ireland; he never made it.

'What's your family name?'

'Connell. Apparently my great grandfather Joe came from these parts. We don't know much about him, except that he liked his whisky, beat my great grandmother up, then scarpered off to New South Wales when my grandfather was a little boy.'

White waves suddenly formed in the window next to Johnny, then hissed as they broke on the shingled shore. The ancient heavy wooden benches of the pub were designed so that you could sit down for a quiet one and stare out to the Atlantic. With its creaks and groans, it felt like you were in a ship.

'Oid say you've come to the right place. There's Connells sprinkled throughout here like gentians around dese parts.'

'Gentians?' I drained my Guinness.

'When you explore da Burren, take a good look in da cracks and crevices. You'll find wild flowers that look like stars, mainly blue and purple. You see, da last Ice Age we had, da Burren sat underneath a giant glacier dat stretched all da way back to the Arctic. Dem flowers came all the way down from the Arctic. There's a whole subterranean world out dere. Da Burren's full of caves and underground streams where tousands of people could live forever. We have *turloughs*, lakes, which are there one day and disappear the next. Dere's one near our lodgings at the moment. Little gobshite, it came from nowhere.' Johnny shouted me a Guinness then rolled himself a cigarette. 'Da Otherworld's a more colourful place dan where these crust-dwellers live.' Johnny pointed his bald shiny dome towards the old fellas. 'Who's round is it, Moike?'

After staggering back from the bar with a pint in each hand, I sat down and rolled myself another cigarette. 'Are you an archaeologist, Johnny?'

'No, more loike local historian. You see, da Burren was a more bustling place than tis today. We were da ones who built the stone forts, dolmens and gallery graves you see all around you, because we wuz always bashin' the shite out of each other. Den we starting facing our forts out to sea because this lot came.' Johnny pointed his pink chubby finger towards the old fellas. 'From Spain. Dat's why you'll find a lot of people out here have de dark features. Anyway, they banished us all to the backwaters, kept all the good land for themselves. Much loike what happened to your Aboriginals. But fek em, we still know how to have a good time. Isn't dat what it's all about?'

As the Aran Isle lighthouse illuminated the pub, the publican shouted last orders.

With a cigarette dangling out of my lips and a belly full of Guinness, I stumbled through the drizzle towards our old bomb of a car, a Datsun 120Y.

I offered Johnny a lift but he told me he didn't believe in cars. I pulled the choke out and watched my new friend dissolve into the darkness. The Datsun coughed and splattered into life.

I heard some traditional music weaving through the night down from the direction of Johnny house. Ah well, it's only some *craic*, I thought. *Craic's* the Irish word for fun or party. There are always good *craic* every night in Ireland. I was tempted to do a U-turn.

A long stretch of purple light trailed across the black sky. In my drunken state, I thought that maybe it was a remnant of the sunset or perhaps it was the northern lights people around here talk about. My eyes tried to focus on the rocky road ahead of me. The Datsun crawled like a snail. All of a sudden on the left side of the road before me, I saw two eyes staring at me, but whatever it was it flew off. My first thought was maybe it was a kid that'd lost its way. I stopped the car, jumped out and shouted, but got no response. Then I saw a shiny object near where the figure had dashed off. I picked it up; it was a tiny pair of golden glasses. I got back into the car and gently placed them on the passenger seat. They're probably toy glasses that have fallen off the kid's doll. Poor kid, I must get help,' I thought.

'There's no Garda station in this town. The only joint that's open now would be Johnny's.' I forgot about the old man's warning and turned the car round. I made out the purple light in my rear-view mirror; it seemed to be pointing the way.

The wind dropped as I made my way up the hill to Johnny's house. I heard the music again. I turned off the main road and slowly made my way across what looked like a rocky driveway. The light of the Aran Isle lit the house up; it seemed smaller from when I saw it from the pub. I heard laughter, singing, a fiddle, *bodhrain*, harp and scores of dancing feet.

I parked the Datsun near a hedge, took the golden glasses of the front seat, straddled the hedge and made my way across the freezing field towards the house. The full moon was a smudge behind racing clouds. Two small muttering figures stood out the back examining a lake next to the house. Nobody was panicking so I figured everything was all right. A light silver mist circled the fields around us.

'Bejesus, you scared the daylights out of us, Aussie,' Johnny said with a big grin as he opened up the door.

The house appeared to be bigger than it was from the outside; it looked like a great hall which seemed to stretch forever. An occasional breath of mist would brush by my cheek. It was full of people the size of toddlers. Johnny had shrunk. Before I knew it, he pointed a hazel wand towards me and I became a midget too!

Johnny gently took me by the arm and escorted me through the buzzing throng of little people towards a golden throne. All the women had long gold or red hair and were dressed in dusk blue or purple gowns. The men were as brightly dressed, favouring red, green or gold shirts with vests. Some of them looked at me in sheer terror, others sneered, some bowed. What I took to be their queen suddenly materialised on the throne. She was taller than the rest, had the same long blonde hair as the others, a body as slim as a sapling and fingers like kindling. She had a golden crown, high cheekbones, wore a long purple gown with aristocratic finery around her shoulders. Her gleaming sky blues were split-pupilled like a cat. All of the little people around me had the same cat eyes.

'I am Morrigan, Queen of the Elven Folk. Welcome, Bard.' Morrigan smiled to reveal pearly white carnivorous teeth.

All was silent except for the lake lapping near the house.

'You are welcome to this gathering, son of Man. Enjoy!' The Queen gestured for the music and dancing to start up again.

'Hey, Johnnie, how did she know I wrote poetry?' I shouted above the din into Johnny's red ear.

'Because we give dem to you bards. You share a reverence for nature like us fairy folk. Man needs to learn to love, especially nature, or we're all doomed.'

'What do you mean, you give them?'

'See dem two gentlemen hovering over what looks like a printing press? They write the first couple of lines for bards, just to kick them off, so to speak, den deliver them.' Johnny pointed towards two little stout fellas all dressed in red, complete with red pointy beards and hats. They both had wings!

I then came to realise that most of the small people around me had wings! The red gentleman on the left was behaving quiet peculiarly. Whatever the machine was they working on, it was big. The little one on the right was doing all right. I'd watch him hover with letters over the thingamajig then drop them into slots. The poor fella on the left was attempting to do the same thing but he kept bumping into the wall, the machine or his workmate. He looked like a drunken butterfly.

'What's wrong with him, Johnny?'

'Da poor man's lost his spectacles. He's as blind as a bat.' Jimmy chuckled.

'What colour were they?' I patted my top pocket.

'Gold. You see, poor old Flann lost his spectacles. After he delivered dat sunset poem to you, he got chased by a badger.' Johnny wet himself as poor Flann kept bumping into obstacles.

'How do they deliver the words to me? I never saw him.'

'A tru da sky messenger – you call 'em birds. You bards know da language of birds. Where there's no birds, there's no poetry.

True enough, I thought, but guilt overtook me. 'Listen, Johnny, I've got his glasses.' I was given a silver goblet of whisky by a beautiful young fairy who had long dark thick hair and very alluring smile. I pinched myself hard: nope, I wasn't dreaming. Here I was in the middle of a fairy gathering in the wilds of Ireland drinking very potent whisky.

'Don't worry, Aussie, I've already figured that.'

'How so? Don't tell me a badger told you?' I was getting a bit cheekier now because I'd just bottomed my second whisky, this time served by a flirty red-haired fairy.

'No, no,' he tittered. 'Flann told me you stopped off near him and rescued his spectacles,' replied Johnny.

'You're not in a hurry for me to return them to Flann?'

'Nope. He's a pompous little fekker and besides it looks so funny.'

I have to admit that after my third glass, Flann did look bloody hilarious.

But I had to give them back to the poor little fella when he was on the verge of tears. He took me over to the gizmo to tell me he'd composed the first few lines to a poem I was going to write tomorrow called Riosin.

'Tell me, Johnny, is Morrigan going to let me go? The locals warned me to keep away from this joint and you know I've read these stories where the fairies take people away forever once there in they're in their clutches.' By this time, I'd lost control of my feet, they were shuffling along to the music.

'Nah, you should be roight, Aussie. We really shouldn't be here. You see, a *turlough* flushed us up to the surface here, but it's receding so we shouldn't be here for dat much longer.' Johnny crinkled his nose. 'And besides, you're not her type.'

'Whaddya mean by that?'

'Morrigan prefers pushovers, not bards, and let's face facts, Aussie, you poets aren't noted for bowing down to anyone.'

'Does that mean I can party on as much as I like?'

'Pretty much.'

The whisky was heavenly; you could drink as much as you like and it made you feel light like a spirit. The fairies get their water from a delta of underground rivers which are fed by the crystal-clear rivers from the nearby mountains.

I threw myself into every dance, whirling and swirling with a succession of beautiful women even if they were three foot tall. I'd got to that blissful stage where I was beyond worry or care. My whole being was inflamed with whisky. I felt incredibly witty, at one stage holding court to a large number of fairies. What I spoke about, I'm buggered if I know.

And then Roisin appeared. She wore a luminous blue dress with the signs of the zodiac; she was the one who served me the first goblet of whisky. With a big smile on her face, she'd pour me another drop as soon as I'd bottomed one. Unlike the women from my home who would put on a cat's bum face nearly every time I had a sip. Again unlike the women at home, she asked me about my poetry. Beautiful Roisin!

She told me her clan originally came from the centre of Ireland and were considered the most royal and fiercest fighters against the invaders. Her dream was for her people to return to the sun. My dream was to stay with her forever. Her breath had the fragrance of water, her blue cat eyes stared right through me. I wanted to run my hand through her thick dark hair. Her shining blue dress was silken and so tight that you could every curve of her wineglass figure. I danced with her for forever until finally the first crimson rays of morning trickled through the windows. Roisin took my by the hand and led me away to her shadowed bedroom with a turf fire.

Stephen found me in the house next day about midday snoring, naked, with my underpants wrapped around my head. The abandoned house was full of dust and cobwebs. The *turlough* had disappeared.

'Roisin, why didn't you take me away?' I cried to myself.

Stephen kept nodding and smiling to himself when I tried to explain to him what had happened the night before. He kept muttering, 'Too much moonshine again Connell.'

I found my clothes neatly folded on a mattress on the floor in what was Roisin's bedroom. Her hearth was stone cold and empty. I lit up my first cigarette and rubbed my forehead. Curiously enough, I didn't have a hangover, just sore eyes due to lack of sleep.

Stephen and I explored the Burren thoroughly that day. We stumbled up rocky hills towards stone rings and gallery graves, portals to the Otherworld. I whispered to Roisin to please take me away. I discovered the tiny town we'd stayed in that night wasn't on the map, and Johnny was right. When we made it to the Aran Isles, the commanding prehistoric fort, Dun Aenges, faced out towards the west, the Atlantic.

That night in Galway, amongst the screaming seagulls, I wrote another poem;

> Roisin
>
> Mists gather within her eyes
> open upon a passionate tide,
> her hair is the shade of She Oak
> teasing my sight with shadowed hope.
> Lapping within her sighs
> build as she thrusts her thighs,
> her neck arches back when she cries
> to clasp upon my fixed desire.

She strokes my hair teases my backbone
curls her body around the fire's glow.
I ponder over her soft long groans
her nakedness below my sweating blows,
how she gave her scented womb to my caress,
a gold chair holds her crumpled blue dress,
restful now we huddle in each others warmth
to slowly drift out of worn harbours of thought.

*

Years later, a *turlough* formed beside a chimney of a house long gone. A dark-haired beauty appeared asking for the whereabouts of her father, 'de Aussie'. None of the locals knew who she was talking about. One of the old fellas in the pub knew of a story where an Aussie had been found naked in a deserted house where the *turlough* now sat. The happening occurred when his grandfather was a little boy, which was about a century ago. With a knowing smile on her face, the dark-haired beauty walked up the barren hill, blew a kiss to the sun then threw herself in to the *turlough*. Her body was never found.

Goodbye 120Y

Stephen's brown eyes have lost their sparkle; we've hardly spoken on our way back to Cork. We're not used to travelling on a bus in the cold and dark. We've just sold our old bomb of a Datsun 120Y. Stephen and I drove over three and half thousand miles in the battered yellow old rust bucket. We journeyed to the most southern, western and northern parts of the republic of Ireland. Now we have to stick to timetables to get around.

Stephen nods when I say it's like experiencing the death of a close friend. We named him after the old Roman emperor from Robert Grave's novel *I Claudius*. My ex bought the book for me as a going away present. We devoured the story as we roamed the Irish countryside and loved yarning about it. Our Datsun turned out to be just like the old emperor: slow, stammered a lot but was reliable once you got him going.

Stephen and I bought him down in the tiny southern town of Clonakilty. We were staying in the nearby village of Timoleague and going for long walks along the coast. The barman in the local pub noticed us going by each day and felt sorry for us. There was no need to, because my mate and I were enjoying our ambles below the blue autumn sky. We'd discovered an ancient forest, then a point at Courtmacsherry from which to stare out at the hazy Celtic Sea and share our love of daydreaming. Our skin developed a healthy golden sheen.

One afternoon, the barman stuck his head out of the front door of the pub and waved at us to come inside. While pouring a couple of pints, he gave us a long talk about how he thought it was a great shame that we didn't have a car to get around in. Stephen shrugged and replied with a Guinness moustache that we probably couldn't afford one. Our ears flapped when the barman said he knew a fellow down the road who would be able to sell us a reasonable car for a couple of hundred pounds. Our heads, being full of sunshine and surf, were open to any suggestion.

I smile wistfully on the bus when I recall the liberating feel of us put-putting off in Claudius. Sure enough, we'd bought him for two hundred quid and the dealer had given us an assurance he'd buy it back for the same price. When Stephen and I tossed our packs into the back seat after discovering the rusted boot lock didn't work, we didn't give a tinker's because it was wonderful not to be lugging those bloody heavy things around on our backs any more.

Claudius had a car radio! One of life's joys is hitting the open road with good company and music blaring out of the speakers. George Harrison belted out his last big hit, 'Got my mind set on you', as Stephen and I chugged off. We were soon to discover why Claudius's cabin was breezy. He had a couple of dirty great big holes in the floor. We rapidly learned to drive with our raincoats on whenever it rained because water would splash up from the highway. We also found that Claudius's windscreen wipers didn't function, which was a bit of a disadvantage because it seemed to rain every second day in Ireland. Oh well, you have to get your priorities right; at least the radio worked.

Claudius refused to start the following morning after we bought him and we couldn't flick the bonnet open because the lever cable was broken. A group of Swiss, German and English backpackers pushed the Datsun down the road and Stephen, despite a coughing engine, managed to jump-start him. From then on, we always parked Claudius on a hill.

One high place I recall was a cliff on the west coast of Ireland. My mate and I pulled up to watch the sun set on the Atlantic Ocean. We were in the middle of a Gaelic-speaking area and the radio played traditional Irish ballads. The combination of ancient haunting chants with a flaring sun that slowly painted the sky and surrounding seascape blood-red, sent shivers up and down my spine. I was in the county my grandfather said our family came from. Stephen eventually jump-started Claudius and we spluttered down the road to find a youth hostel in the middle of nowhere. We had the place to ourselves. Stephen built a peat fire while I bought some Guinness. We were joined by two ginger pussy cats who we christened Augustus and Livia. It was a perfect night of studying the flames, purring lap cats, drinking, talking and laughter. I sighed on the bus and wondered if we'd ever get the opportunity to visit such a remote place again.

As we made out the lights of Cork in the distance, Stephen told me the dealer in Clonakilty was an arsehole. The mongrel dog only gave us eighty pounds for Claudius. I suppose money-grubbers are the same the world over.

This is our last night in the south. We've decided to catch the train to Dublin and then push on to Belfast.

Another reason we sold Claudius is that security's a lot tighter in the north. We've been told a car from the republic would be targeted by the authorities and we'd find ourselves in a spot of bother once it was discovered that Claudius wasn't insured or roadworthy. Some people in Timoleague also recommended that my friend and I get a haircut and beard trim because we look like a couple of IRA gunrunners.

Security is different in the south. Stephen and I happened to travel through the republic during a kidnapping. The Gardai (Irish police) and army were out in full force. We believed we could escape detection by avoiding the main roads and towns. Little did we know that the IRA probably thought the same way too. We drove into a dozen roadblocks. Stephen would always answer yes when asked if the car was insured and roadworthy. He'd answer no when they'd ask us to open the boot. At one roadblock Claudius creaked into, there was a soldier accompanying the Gardai decked out in camouflage and wielding a machine gun. It was the first time I'd seen someone with a face smudged black and branches sprouting out of his helmet.

He asked us to step out of the car. 'Is the car insured, boys?'

'Yes,' lied Stephen.

I was paralysed by honest fear.

'Is the car roadworthy, boys?'

'Yep,' my mate bullshitted again.

'Can you open the boot?'

'Um, no.'

'And why's that then?'

'Because the lock's rusted.'

'Would you mind me having a look, lads?'

When the soldier came up to us, Stephen handed him the keys. He tried the lock with one hand. Claudius refused to budge. The soldier leant his machine gun beside the old Datsun and had a go with both hands.

After a lot of groaning and grunting, one of the blue-uniformed Gardai took over. When he got nowhere as well, he turned to us with a twinkle in his eye. 'Where are you boys from? Oh, Australia! Drive on boys, drive on.' He threw us back the keys.

Maybe that's the real reason why Stephen and I are down. Tomorrow we're crossing the border into the unknown and know we'll miss the generosity of the Irish. We've spent months travelling through a country that felt like home. Stephen and I were offered endless drinks, genuine conversation, a place to stay for the night and sometimes even a lend of a car. We shared an irreverent sense of humour. After a close footy match in Killarney, the locals insisted on taking us back to the pub to celebrate Australia defeating Ireland. On the other side of the planet, we've discovered our roots and don't really want to leave. Oh well, we all have to leave home sometimes. Let's see what Belfast has in store for us.

The Burren

This was the last part of the county to explore. Kathryn had been told that somewhere around here lay the bones of her great grandmother. She shivered as the lunar landscape opened up around her. Brendan pointed his skinny hand across to a handful of deserted cottages on the crest of a distant grey hill.

The youth hostel was a run-down manor house. It had a note on the front door saying the owner was away, but travellers were still welcome to stay. Kathryn staggered upstairs, crossed a ward lined with bunk beds then tossed her pack onto the bed closest to the bay window. She dragged a lounge chair across the wood floor towards the window to collapse into what felt like the softest cushion of her journey. She listened to the hissing ocean.

Kathryn saw Brendan march down a trail that led to the beach. A bloated sun was plunging into the Atlantic. Red flares of sunlight flooded the horizon. An image of her Auntie Dolly suddenly came into Kathryn's mind. Silver-haired Auntie Dolly was bouncing a tiny Kathryn on her skeletal knee, her warbling voice telling Kathryn she should be proud to have bushranger blood coursing through her veins. Auntie Dolly's uncle was Joe Byrne, Ned Kelly's lieutenant.

She struggled on her aunt's lap when she was shown sepia photographs taken of Joe the day after they killed him. His body was strung up like a puppet; his hands were scorched by the fire that burnt down Glenrowan Inn. Those charred fingers had once scrawled a defence of the Kelly gang, and written ballads for the little people. Those fleshy stumps had squeezed the trigger to blow away his old mate, Aaron, to Christ knows where.

Hazy memories, dead Auntie Dolly's unfulfilled dream to get back to County Clare. Kathryn had forked out many a pound note to spend the day sifting through birth and death certificates. She and a silent Brendan had explored graveyards dotted with weeping angels and Celtic crosses, to find no record of the Byrnes.

Brendan hunched over an open fire, slurping and stirring a pot of soup. Red embers flared each time the Arctic wind rushed down the chimney. His glazed eyes mirrored the flames as he murmured away to himself. A yawning, stretching Kathryn suddenly floated through the doorway. She quietly knelt down next to the flames.

'G'day, sleepy head. How's it going?' Brendan's weather-beaten face crinkled when he smiled.

'I've had the best sleep of our trip. No snoring or smelly-armpit tourist disturbed me. How was it down there?' Kathryn yawned again.

'It was bloody amazing. The sun reflected off the mountains and sea, everything merged into red. I've still got blind spots in front of my eyes. I wrote four poems while you slept.' Brendan rubbed the black stubble on his chin. He leant down towards Kathryn and began to stroke her long dark hair. 'Your ears are on fire. It's what's-his-face. He's sending words, twelve thousand miles across the ocean. He's saying come back home to the nest of wealth-acquiring drones.'

'Just leave it, eh? I'm over here with you. Isn't that enough, for God's sake?' Kathryn took a swig from Brendan's Guinness bottle.

He chuckled then turned back to nurse the soup.

A lighthouse from an island across the sea suddenly lit up. Their room flared with white light at regular intervals. Kathryn sipped Brendan's soup. She recalled the way David, her husband, squirmed on the edge of the couch when confronted with the Byrne family for the first time. His puzzled 'You understand that gobbledygook?' after Kathryn translated her sister's toddler language for him. She thought of David's snooty response to Kathryn's father, Brian, who chain-smoked and nattered about the gee-gees. She remembered the silence of the streets of Templestowe, after the swarm of voices at the Housing Commission estate. And David, always outside when the Byrnes visited, pretending to do renovations to their house that looked like a Masonic lodge.

Brendan nodded towards the window. 'That's the Aran Isle out there.'

Kathryn looked up to see the island's cottage lights trace fluid trails on the black sea.

Brendan scoured his dog-eared map. 'I reckon this town we're in is Fanore, Katie.'

Kathryn remembered how she'd rediscovered her childhood friend, Brendan, sleeping in a bus stop in Templestowe. He was living like a gypsy and studying literature, in a decayed old weatherboard cottage on the back blocks of one of the last orchards. 'Stuffed if I know,' was his response when she asked him what he wanted to do with his degree.

'Listen!' Brendan suddenly shouted one night to David and Kathryn. His brown eyes were wild with excitement. The melody of a willy wagtail drifted through their dining room window. Brendan went out to the front nature strip to sit below an old man gum tree. Kathryn followed him.

'This place used to be teeming with these little fellas, until those bastard developers came along and pulled every tree down. Look after him, Kathryn, eh? He's the last of his mob.'

The dancing bird sang beneath a canopy of stars. They sat outside for hours, talking and watching the north wind brush the night sky. David's television threw its blue sheen along the marble hallway behind the screen door.

Kathryn floated in and out of sleep. Sometimes she'd see the peat collapse into grey mounds of soot. At one stage she saw a silhouette squatting in front of the fire. 'Is that you, Bren?' Kathryn leaned up. The shade turned to face her. Kathryn sensed it was female. It silently went back to study the dying fire.

'You remember your dreams once you're away from work,' Brendan said to her the next day.

Their old bomb of a car put-putted up a rocky ridge. His dark eyes stared up at the sun, which was a faint orange smudge behind a wall of mist. 'Last night I dreamt I stepped up into the sky. I felt I had springs on my shoes. I soared over a flat grey landscape. I felt strangely detached as I flew like a phantom towards a yellow smoking sun. That detachment's been haunting me all morning.'

Kathryn's forehead wrinkled. She stared at rocks that squatted like sentinels on top of a distant hill. A nearby cottage merged into a broth of low-lying cloud.

'Turn right up here. I reckon that's the ring fort, jutting out like a pimple on the edge of that mountain.' Brendan tossed his map into the back seat.

Kathryn turned the car to crawl along a white road full of ruts. Rain bands swept in from the powder blue ocean.

Brendan and Kathryn resembled a pair of monks while they staggered around the walls of the ring fort in their black raincoats.

'What can you see, Bren?' she shouted through the wind.

He didn't reply. A burst of rain forced Kathryn back into the car. When she last saw Brendan, he was leaning down to poke his head into the beginning of an underground passageway.

Kathryn squinted through the streaming windscreen towards the figure of someone slowly coming towards the car. It was an old man shuffling along a stone path; she could just make out his ancient black cap and oak walking stick. His clay-coloured face looked like it had been chiselled out of the local rock.

He raised his stick towards the car, then muttered in a sing-song voice, 'Hello, lass. You look like you're a long ways from home. What brings you here?'

'We're exploring the fort.' Kathryn wound down the car window.

'Oh, me fort. Oh well, you're most welcome to have a look around.'

As she stepped out of the car, the old man slowly turned his watery blue eyes to the now clearing sky and uttered, 'We're standing in the belly of a glacier, lass.'

'What do you mean?' Kathryn peered towards a band of mist that had enveloped the ring fort. Brendan wasn't around.

'During the old days, a glacier stretching hundreds of miles from the north, sat here like a white giant, carving out the Burren. There's still some Arctic flowers to be found. If you spot blue star-shaped wild flowers perching in the rock shelves, you'll know that's them.'

> 'The Burren, The Burren,
> where the green roads do run,
> over hill, over dale they sing
> tales of the magical ring.'

The ditty her father used to sing in the shower suddenly popped into her mind. Kathryn studied the old man's face while he spoke; he had the same huge brow and square head she'd seen in photographs taken of her great grandfather in Melbourne, after he'd stepped of the boat from Ireland.

'My name's Kathryn Byrne.'

'Mine's Tom O'Loughlan. How do you do, child?'

'Do you know any Byrnes in this neck of the woods?'

'No. Most of them left for the New World many moons ago.'

Jesus, Kathryn thought to herself, I've searched everywhere in this God-forsaken county, not finding one member of my bloody family. Was Aunty Dolly right, or was she a notorious yarn spinner like all the Byrnes?

Sensing her disappointment, the old man mumbled, 'Doesn't matter anyways, child. Home is where the heart is.'

Brendan suddenly appeared out of nowhere, jumping over a maze of potholes towards them. Yellow strips of sunlight chased shadows over the silver ridges behind him.

'So what do you think of our Burren? A lot of travellers hate this place.'

'It reminds me of the desert country where I was born.' Brendan's curly black hair blew in the wind. 'I love the stillness…the only thing you hear is the sound of the wind whistling through stone.'

A wren hovered overhead; its intense medley wove through their conversation. They finally parted company when another wall of dark cloud loomed nearby.

'Looks like a black wind's on her way,' warned Tom as they said their farewell.

'Did you hear Tom call the wren the king of all birds?'

Kathryn shook her head.

'That's because they reckon he was in a competition with all the other birds to see who could fly the highest. He hitched a ride on the back of a stronger bird. When the other bird tired, the wren soared off and beat everybody else. I admire the little fella.' Brendan put his rainbow-coloured beanie on his head.

A sudden downpour of rain clattered on the roof of their car.

'Old Tom reminded me of your granddad, Katie, the way he'd point out things to us. Like the night he told us, when we were little kids, that magpies are the spirits of our dead relatives. Or if you look hard enough, you can see the face of God in a full moon.'

Kathryn thought of how David used to ridicule her every time she tried to share her grandfather's insights with him.

The Atlantic droned as Brendan crawled out of their bed. She watched his huddled shadow merge into the darkness of the doorway. His thoughts were of the afternoon, and how he'd managed to crawl into a tiny chamber of the ring fort. Brendan recalled when he knelt down and placed his ear on the ancient fortress wall to listen to the wind's tune. He made out his book in the crimson light. Brendan tossed more peat onto the fire. The flames caressed away the chill in his fingers. He sat and watched the moonlight revealing the outline of a distant peninsula. The Aran Isle lighthouse illuminated the pages of his book; Brendan composed a poem.

Kathryn spent the next morning in Ennis. 'B, B, bloody B,' she muttered while she thumbed through yellow cardboard records of the families of Clare. 'Barrett, Boyle, Brady.' Flick went the cards under her angry hands. 'Buckley, Burns. God where are you? I've blown another twenty quid on these useless bloody records. Butler, Byrne! Resident of Fanore!'

'So this is it, eh?' a gasping Brendan asked as they staggered up a nearby hill.

The clay-coloured ocean below them churned.

'The graveyard's behind these empty cottages you pointed to when we first came into Fanore.'

They walked past the shattered homes and stumbled through a stone ring, towards a clump of weather-beaten tombstones. The rain and wind had defaced the inscriptions.

'She's supposed to be here somewhere, Mary Byrne!' Images of her dead relatives swirled around her head. Her giggly grandmother, Leila, with her generous kisses, the way she'd talk through her nose when she'd had a bit to drink.

('You do the same, Katie,' Brendan once observed.)

Her bull-headed grandfather, Alan, splashing around their backyard pool chasing Kathryn's little sister, unaware his exposed testicles were dangling out of his shorts. The way her grandfather used to call David a Methodist wowser. The hurt look on Alan's face when she once angrily replied, 'I married him because he's a gentleman, not a pig like you and your bloody son.'

'Doesn't matter, Katie.' Brendan took his beanie off. 'Unlike my family, the important thing is you found her.'

'No, I haven't. You can't read the tombstones. I don't know which one she is.'

'Yes, but you know her spirit's here.'

A cormorant dived into the ocean below her. The Burren mountains began to slowly turn from a rust colour into silver. The wind blew through Brendan's hair while he picked a handful of tiny blue flowers and sprinkled them over the graves. Kathryn rubbed the knot in her stomach.

She leant into the jet's window. The coastal city's light reminded her of an amoeba. The neon glow was eventually swallowed by the darkness of the Indian Ocean. Kathryn looked at her watch to realise that

Brendan would be flying over southern England towards London to find work. She lifted her feet off the cold floor and tucked them under her thighs. Kathryn leant back and stared into the black belly of the sleeping jumbo. Already her journey to the Burren with her absent friend was starting to feel like a dream.

The jet banked. She opened a book she'd bought in Ennis. A blue gentian and a foolscap page fell onto her lap. She stroked the flower and squinted through the cabin light to read Brendan's poem:

> Wind Gifts
>
> Moonlight straddles the edge
> of the dark peninsula,
> curling ribbons of white
> swell to break this leaden darkness.
> Waxing winds coil through
> the shattered shore stones, hissing
> tidal songs coldly brew
> behind our glowing faces leaning
> for relief into the flaring hearth:
> whistling tunes flow from our thawing hearts.

Kathryn sent 'Wind Gifts' off to publishers. It took a couple of years to get into print. Brendan never replied to her letter announcing the good news. The last she ever heard of him, he was working in a cannery somewhere along the Dingle Peninsula. She'd kept her promise to him not to return to David. She remembered the shrieking seagulls as he waved from the ferry taking him to the Aran Isle. She recalled his brown face merging into the purple light of dusk. He'll soon lose that sad look on his face, she told herself; not realising it was the last time she'd see him.

Stuff It

Out of the blue, I was invited to be Nigel Stoop's best man. We went to school donkey's years ago but had barely kept in contact. The poor bugger never registered any of my piss-weak hints that I didn't want to keep in contact with him. Poor old Nigel, the school's punching bag. The tall weed with the thick glasses, likeable enough, but had the intellectual depth of a tadpole pond.

The main thing that shitted me about Nigel was that he was such a boring fart; all he wanted to talk about was money. Nigel's old man, Bob, was a CUB (cashed-up bogan) who lived in this huge McMansion in Doncaster. Nigel used to ask me questions like 'How much money has your father got in the bank? How come you live in such a tiny little wooden dump? Why does your father drive around in that old shitcan of a Morris Minor?'

'Stuffed if I know,' and 'I don't give a rat's arse,' were my standard answers to his sticky-beaking.

I was a 'Chaddy boy', born and raised in working-class Chadstone, where everyone was so busy working their backsides off they didn't have time to indulge in being capos. I hated it when the fam moved to the more affluent side of town. Besides, I was also a dreamy-headed teenager more interested in D and M conversations and as a result was labelled a wanker or a smart-arse by the non-reflective of our school.

'G'day, Mike. Wadda youse reckon? I reckon you'll be the bestest best man ever. It'll be a humungus piss up. I've hired a couple of kegs.'

'I don't know, Nigel.' Jesus Harry! How do I pike out of this one? I thought, as I recognised his familiar bogan accent over the dog and bone. 'I think I may have something else on that night.' (Like the telly, I wanted to tell him.)

'Whaddya mean you think youse may have something else on,

you dickhead! Just bloody well cancel it, mate. Christ, you and I have known each other for yonks. C'mon, you useless prick! Besides, my sister Pam's going to be a bridesmaid and she always reckoned you're a bit of a spunk.'

'Pam, eh ?' I have to admit that with her bottle-blonde hair and lovely long legs, I always considered Nigel's sister to be a bit of a hornbag.

Before I knew it, I was sitting in Nigel's folk's backyard around a brick barbecue, trapped in the primal ritual of a buck's night. Pam was nowhere to be seen, bugger it! I found out later on that she was at Nigel's other half's hens' night. Lying bastard! He'd said that to suck me in.

'Help yourselves to the mystery bags and dead horse, boys.' Nigel's old man's grill sizzled away; with his mullet haircut and David Boon moustache, Bob had hardly altered at all.

'So you haven't bit the dust like me, eh Mikey? You still on your Pat Malone?' Nigel placed his arm around my shoulder.

'Yeah, I want to travel while I'm still a spring chicken. Actually, I've just come back from Ireland.'

'Fucking Ireland!' The groomsman, Gary 'Ebbo' Evans, ripped the lid off his esky.

I'd forgotten all about this tonk. Gary, known for his rapier-like wit, was Nigel's best cobber at school.

'Whatya wanna go to a shit dump like that for, full of fucking Micks and terrorists?' He stared at me through his glazed ferret-like eyes. The lights were on but nobody was home.

Before I had the right of reply, Ebbo handballed a stubby to everyone then gave us all a full run-down of his epic trail bike trek from Dandenong to Echuca. The story went for ages over a series of belches and stubbies. Nigel and the gang were held spellbound. I was bored shitless and watched the bugs crackle in Mr Stoop's mozzie zapper.

'Whaddya do for a crust these days, Mikey, me old mate?' Nigel spluttered towards midnight.

'Um…I'm a freelance journalist.'

'A fucking journo!' Ebbo guzzled down his beer. 'I reckon they spend most of their time with their hands on their dicks. I suppose you're in one of those pinko rags who hates Tony Abbot, eh? I love old Abbot. When he makes up his mind, he bloody well sticks to it, no matter what. He get things done, he doesn't take any shit from no one. At least you know where you stand with him.'

'Yeah, just like old Adolf, eh?' I sipped my drink.

Ebbo gave me a look to kill.

'I'll vote for anyone who fights against those useless Greenies,' muttered a flannel shirt wearer from out of the shadows.

'The weather's stuffed. Where have all the old Melbourne winters gone, eh? You remember the May holidays where it seemed to rain forever? Remember summer, where you always had a cool change after four days of heat? It's not just us too. The weather system around the world has gone down the dunny. The trouble with all the pollies is they have a big wankfest but they do sweet Fannie Adams. Abbot's only behaving like Mr Action man to suck in shit-for-brains like you. I mean, apart from favours to his rich mates, he's been in politics for yonks but what's he actually done, eh? Just exposed his small business stimulation package in his budgie smugglers!'

'Good on ya, Nigel.' I patted him on the back as he sat back down next to me. I was having a hard enough time as it was, so I decided to get snakes hissed with the Neanderthals. At least grog deadens the pain. Someone put Barnsey on.

The night dragged on. I went over to have a yarn with Mr Stoops but only muttered a few monosyllables then went inside to watch the footy. I forgot that he hated Collingwood supporters. Ebbo gave us a detailed account on how to replace worn pistons on a '69 Monaro.

'You know Monaro's an Aboriginal word for big breasts,' I laughed and took a swig on my beer. 'You could just imagine all these chief executives in Detroit saying, 'Hey let's play a trick on those dumb-assed Aussies and call their car big tits.'

'You calling me a dumb arse?' Ebbo spat at me.

'Why don't you shut the fuck up for a change, Ebbo. Christ, you're a boring bag of bullshit sometimes.' Nigel stood to poke the groomsman on the chest.

'Oooooohooh!' came the yobbo chant of the bandaged knuckle brigade around me.

'Ooohooh! Nigel's getting a bit tetchy because he thinks he won't be able to crack a fat tomorrow night.' Ebbo cracked another beer.

'Get fucked, prick! Now, Mike, tell us how you went walkabout around Ireland.'

As the flames reflected on Nigel's glasses, it twigged that he was trying to give me a go. Jesus Harry! Was I wrong about him or what? I spoke for a sec then they all started singing, 'The last plane out of Sydney's almost gone'. You bloody beauty!

'Khe Sanh's a fucking classic!' Ebbo took a packet of Winfields out of his shirtsleeves and offered me one.

'You're not wrong there, Gary.' I smiled at him as I lit up a fag.

Stuff it! The night mightn't turn out to be so shithouse after all, I reckon.

The Cyclist

Michael stared through the white sunlight streaming outside the train window. The train had pulled into Blackburn station. He squinted as he made out the outline of a schoolgirl. She had on a royal blue blazer, with a thick blue tunic. Her hair was black and shoulder length, her skin pale. She was making obscene gestures towards him. A shadow was over her face, yet Michael could make out white grimacing teeth. She was sitting cross-legged upon the station bench.

The train slowly started moving away from her. Two schoolboys sitting next to him sniggered as they returned their two-fingered salutes towards the defiant girl.

The sun squatted silver behind thin grey clouds of summer morning. Michael remembered staring at a similar white flaring sun when he was a kid in a school playground. His mother would always warn him that he would burn his eyes out if he kept that up. He continued to do it. It was his secret: there was something enticing and mysterious about staring into the chalk face of a forbidden sun.

Music drifted through the ear pieces of his Walkman. Michael sat with his elbow on the edge of the train window and studied the suburban landscape rushing past him.

It was his thirty-eighth birthday. An hour ago he'd been lying on his back in bed while his wife Caitlin stroked his round stomach wishing him happy birthday. She had given him a train set; she had heard stories of when he was a young kid how he'd always manage to break train sets given to him by his parents in a rush of enthusiasm while trying to construct them. Caitlin figured there was a good chance that history wouldn't repeat itself this time. Michael cackled to himself picturing him and his wife that night, watching the train going around in endless circles.

An image of a schoolgirl in a clay brown uniform, peddling her push bike suddenly dropped into his mind. Vicki…Vicki Coughlan; she had the same pearl-white teeth as the schoolgirl in Blackburn. She used to ride her bike over the Yarra each day and visit him when he worked in the plant nursery. It was his first job after he had failed HSC. He remembered her being happy for him finding a job after being unemployed for months. Michael couldn't share her enthusiasm; he was depressed after seeing all his close friends going off to university. He recalled her shoulder-length red hair, her creamy skin, the small sprinkling of freckles below her hazel eyes, and her willowy teenage body. Her joyfulness would momentarily drag him out of his self-pitying mood.

Although Michael was only a couple of years older than Vicki, he used to feel he was light years away from her. Vicki went to St Brigit's private school in Heidelberg. She used to ride her bike everywhere, looking like a little brown hunchback as she plodded through suburban streets. Whereas Michael saw himself as a man of the world, having experienced the rough and tumble of a government school. Besides, he was a working man, on the threshold of buying a car.

As the train sped forward, Michael noticed yellow bands of smog sitting over the grey city horizon. His mind turned further back to the days when he used to work for Venture Stores part-time after school. He was put in charge of the record section of the store, and as a result saw himself as a bit of a dude.

Vicki used to visit him; they'd talk about music. She pointed out to him that Jethro Tull's *Warchild* album used Melbourne as a backdrop. A picture of the front cover of the album came into Michael's memory: the night skyline of Melbourne in 1974, a purple city lit up by hellish red lights sitting behind a ghostly blue wizard image of the lead singer. He recalled how Vicki use to rock and sway her little body to the frenetic music of *Warchild*. He adored the words 'I'll write on your tombstone, and thank you for dinner' from the song 'Bungle In the Jungle'. God, he hadn't heard that song for ages.

The train descended into the underground loop. A powdered-faced woman passenger sitting across from him stretched out her newspaper. A headline announced the death of two further people due to heat exhaustion. Michael mind went back further to when he was still at school, to a summer night when he and his friend Robbie met Vicki and her friend walking around the streets of Bulleen. Vicki was holding up her friend, who was tipsy and giggly. Robbie suggested that they all go back to his house, as his parents weren't home.

Robbie and…? Christ, what was her name? Robbie and *Lisa* were pashing on something terrible. Michael sat awkwardly on his chair sucking a beer; Vicki was silent, staring at the neon street light humming outside. Michael rode feelings of jealousy and disgust towards the now recumbent couple slobbering on a straining beanbag somewhere in the shadows before him.

'Hey, Vick, do you want to go out in the yard?'

'Yeah,' came her quiet reply through the darkness.

Michael unbuttoned his shirt and lit up a cigarette in an attempt to look cool as they staggered through the passageway towards the outside. Once at the back door, Michael groped forever in the darkness trying to find the handle. They finally made it out into the backyard to sit below a dry pine tree; its silhouette appeared like a shroud of a pyramid against the blue pulsating summer stars.

He recalled that Vicki pointed out how the neighbours' huge white gum tree appeared to be luminous in the moonlight; she always loved the phrase 'ghost gum'. She told the teenage Michael that when she was a little girl she'd spook herself at night by looking out the window at her father's ghost gum tree, convinced it was haunted.

Michael desperately tried to remember what else they spoke about that night. He pictured his arm around her lithe shoulders as they talked, and how sheer awkwardness prevented him from trying anything further. He recalled how she was terrified by the horror of a nuclear war, and how her little body shivered as she described buildings and houses flattened and scorched by missiles.

Michael was haunted by the same nightmare as a kid. He would go visit his uncle and immerse himself in his relatives' huge library, poring over anything to do with war. The more he read, the more he was convinced that nuclear war wouldn't break out. 'Russia's bottled up in Eastern Europe, Vicki, and China's not gunna take over the planet. The Communists hate each other's guts, China and Russia have had huge border fights, which the Western press haven't talked about. China had a war with India in the sixties where they thrashed the pants off them, but they didn't push on to Delhi or anything like that. The Vietnam War's finished, thank God.'

Michael felt a shudder through Vicki's bird-like body.

She leant over to stroke his eyelids and asked, 'Are you a philosopher?'

Michael blew out of his beer, 'Buggered if I know!'

'I think you're a philosopher, Michael.'

Michael switched on his computer and sat down for another day in the office as the phone rang.

'G'day mate. How are you?

Michael was seldom given the chance to respond. Wouldn't you like to know, he thought to himself. He remembers once telling the other person on the line that he was depressed; the enquirer didn't hear him.

'I'm well. How are you?' Yes sir, no sir, three bags full sir. Eek, eek, throw pennies in the cup for the performing monkey with the curly tale, fez and vest. Eek, fucking eek, all fucking day.

Michael was anxious to tell one of his workmates about Vicki, but the busy madness of the day swept everything aside. He remembered how after that night, he spent years chasing after another woman to get nowhere fast. Vicki slowly faded out of his life as he changed jobs, studied at night school, gained entrance into university, then ended up working as a labourer on a farm in Tasmania. He flew back to Melbourne when he heard his uncle had prostate cancer.

Michael never forgot the look on his uncle's face when he visited him in hospital: it was a jaundice face drained of any emotion. His uncle's chin was clenched hard, his grey eyes lifeless. Michael's aunt attempted small talk and humour towards her husband; he didn't respond.

'You should piss off back to Tassie, Michael. There's nothing for you here,' murmured the voice of his uncle. 'Take my books and boots with you, eh?'

Michael went off for a smoke.

He thought he saw Vicki's friend walking up a corridor towards him. 'Christ!' Michael spluttered. 'I haven't seen you for donkey's – it's been about ten years. How are you? How's Vicki?'

The woman's dark brown eyes shot him a look of hatred, 'What do you mean?' she spat back.

Michael reeled back, 'I dunno. I'm just asking a question.'

'What do you mean? Haven't you heard?'

'Heard what? I've been living in Tasmania for a few years. We hardly hear anything about Melbourne down there.'

'The accident. It was in the papers,' she replied.

'What accident?'

'Vicki's dead. Didn't you hear about that woman who was crushed when a chimney fell down on her?'

'Vaguely. Wasn't it during her birthday, her twenty-first or something?'

'Yeah, that was Vicki. The loft chimney collapsed in her flat. It crushed her. It didn't kill anyone else, just her.' Her eyes fixed viciously on Michael. 'Everyone was dancing to loud music, the chimney was loose, apparently the arsehole of a landlord had known about it for years, but had done fuck all, the prick. Didn't you know?'

'As I said before, I've been living down in Tassie, working my bum off. It's been great…'

She walked off as he blubbered on.

The train began to slowly rise along the backbone of a hill. The dark blue mountains of the Great Dividing Range wearily loomed through the smoky yellow haze of dusk. Michael mulled over in his mind on how these mountains were carved and flattened by the endless cycle of a furnace summer.

The train crawled past Box Hill cemetery; the multitude of granite graves shimmered in a snaking curtain of heat waves. Michael noticed that some of the headstones appeared to be leaning away from the merciless rays of the setting sun. Michael wondered if Vicki, wherever she was, felt relief now that the night had come. The night. What if he'd been there on the night of Vicki's birthday? They might have danced together, shared a few drinks. She might have been standing somewhere else.

As the train took off from Blackburn, Michael silently cursed, wishing that he had returned some sort of gesture towards the blue-uniformed schoolgirl in the morning.

Caitlin shouted him a meal in his favourite restaurant that night. She fingered the rim of her wine glass, sometimes looking over her drink to focus on Michael's distant blue eyes. He ranted as he resurrected his story about Vicki.

'For heaven's sake, Michael, lighten up. It's your birthday,' Caitlin pleaded, 'Why do we have to talk about her, anyway? It's so depressing!'

'All right, all right,' he muttered. He poured himself the last of the wine as the waitress arrived with their meal.

Michael's mind wandered as they quietly ate amidst the chatter of others in the restaurant. He surveyed the dead-eyed diners and wondered if he looked like them. If in the process of becoming an adult, he had ceased to be the young philosopher Vicki once observed. Was she right, or was Caitlin right to say that he was depressing to be around? All he understood at the moment was that Vicki should have lived longer, and that he was living less.

Michael looked across at Caitlin. She was stone-faced. 'Look, I'm sorry, Cat. Thanks for the meal. It's really good…really.'

Later on that night, Caitlin went to bed early while Michael slowly assembled the train set. He shut the lounge room door, turned off the lights and watched as the little locomotive's headlight wove continuous white circles through the summer darkness.

The Shearwater

It was four in the morning and Kathy was still awake; the ocean had roared all night. She was sure that any minute now a wave was going to smash through the window. Kathy nudged Simon; his slow breathing threatened to break into a snore. He growled something before tossing over onto his side. Lightning flashed through the crack between the blind and the window frame.

A gust of wind burst into their room, the blind flicked over a bedside lamp. Simon sprang up and cursed his way towards the window, slammed it shut, then groped through the dark to find the bed again. As he slid below the blankets, he made out Kathy's long, thin silhouette. She was lying on her back with her eyes wide open. He heard her swallowing repeatedly. Simon stroked her forehead. Thunder murmured somewhere in the distance. Her mind was struggling with the idea of having a child. Simon drifted back to sleep.

Kathy leant up to look out of the window. The lighthouse swept its silver beam through a thick spray. Blue sheet lightening flickered out on the ocean. They'd driven hundreds of miles away from the city that afternoon. She remembered how their spirits rose when they sped over Tower Hill and saw the familiar Portmagee peninsula jutting out into the ocean. She recalled the shine in Simon's blue eyes while he pointed to the giant heads of Norfolk pine looming over the white afternoon haze. They felt like they'd stepped back through time when they cruised through Portmagee's wide streets dotted with bluestone cottages. Kathy leant back onto her pillow to see the street light form cross patterns upon the trickling windowpane. The storm eased.

Simon stepped out onto the front porch to watch the remnants of last night's gloom dissolve below the rising sun. The sky became a pyramid of purple clouds. Nearby sand dunes glowed in gold light. He placed a hot pot of tea next to his chair and sat down to write some lyrics. His band had been gigging around Melbourne for ten years now. Simon was the chief songwriter. He'd once told Kathy that composing was the only thing between him and insanity.

Kathy rose a few hours later. They decided to go for a walk along the sea to the lighthouse.

A silver-bearded man with piercing green eyes greeted then in the main street. He was the owner of the second-hand bookshop who, no matter what the weather, always sported a yellow cravat below his grey tweed jacket. 'Hello, you two. You're like the shearwaters the way you turn up every September.' The old man lifted his black beret off his bald head.

'Have they arrived yet, Ted?' Simon ran his fingers through his thinning red hair.

'As regular as clockwork. They always ride the trade winds to arrive on the twenty-second of September. They go back to the same burrow they dug out the year before. The birds do this huge figure of eight pattern as they fly all the way over to the Aleutian Islands and back without any landfall. It's good to know there's a cycle of life out there that carries on regardless of what man does. It helps put things into perspective, don't you think?'

'Bloody oath! The storm was unbelievable last night. Did the town suffer any damage?' Simon stared at a dark wall of clouds racing in from the sea.

'I hope so. Yesterday afternoon I watched as a solitary black cloud decide to park itself just outside of town. It threw down a bolt of lightning. Next came a huge explosion which shook the whole township. It played havoc with the power supply. It melted a few phones and computers. It's given people here something to think and talk about rather than themselves. I believe it was him upstairs reminding us that he's still around… Must go now. Someone's strolled into my shop. Hope to see you at the Caledonian tonight for a few refreshers.' Ted pointed to Simon.

'We'll be there with bells on, won't we, Kath? Simon linked his fingers into Kathy's outstretched hand. The couple walked out of town.

'September the twenty-second's the spring equinox. God, they're amazing critters, those birds, Kath. I'm so looking forward to seeing my mates again.' Simon laughed to himself.

Kathy remembered the year before, when they spotted a swirling dark cloud near the lighthouse at dusk. As they walked closer to investigate, they realised the sky was teeming with shearwaters. Thousands of birds swept in silent circles around them. An excited Simon crouched down in the sand, pulled out his ever-present exercise book from his coat and began to write. She recalled the joyful look on his face when he stared up into the dimming sky.

They spent the middle of the day exploring the island near the lighthouse. The storm had dredged the ocean into a red colour. Rain shadows raked the horizon as they collected shells and pebbles on the shore. A burst of horizontal rain forced Simon and Kathy to shelter below a Norfolk pine.

Kathy's thoughts churned. He asked her if she was all right. She told him she was tired from last night's storm.

They fought the wind as they headed back towards town. Kathy pointed to a seabird bobbing like a duck below a nearby sea wall. It looked like a large seagull; it was trying to use the rising tide to gain a foothold on the sea wall rocks. Sometimes the bird managed to crawl into a hole in the sea wall only to be flushed out by the rising waves. As they walked closer, Simon recognised the black wings and tube-like beak.

'It's a shearwater,' he cried out. 'Looks like her wing's broken.'

Kathy slowly edged her way down the sea wall, plucked the bird out of the water without a struggle, and placed it in another hole, only to see it forced out again by the rising waves.

Simon ran over to a nearby Department of Conservation sign only to find it had no contact phone number. 'Fucking typical!' he muttered.

By now, Kathy was walking towards him, nursing the exhausted bird in her arms.

'Let's take it to the vet.' Simon gestured towards the town.

Kathy nodded. Her moist blue eyes were wide open. Her cheeks stung as they rushed back into Portmagee.

The vet was closed. Simon rang the after-hours number.

'No worries,' came the voice over the phone. 'Trouble is, you'll have to bring the bird to our surgery in Warrnambool.'

Simon replied that he didn't care about the distance, so long as the bird got attention.

They flew along the coast road. The shearwater hardly moved except to groan every time the car hit a bump. Simon agonised over whether he should keep speeding or slow down. The bird's eyes were slowly closing over. Kathy said she could still feel a heartbeat. Now and then, the bird attempted to crawl out of her arms. Whenever it struggled, Kathy pouted her lips, and repeatedly whispered, 'You'll be all right, sweetie.' Simon pictured in his mind the silhouette of the bird skimming over the Pacific from one hemisphere to the other. The skin on his skull tightened as the shearwater's head drooped.

Five square-headed yobbos in a car behind them hurled abuse when Simon suddenly swerved his car into the vet's driveway. Kathy and Simon stood in the brightly lit waiting room where a moronic voice shouted out from a radio about why his Warrnambool car yard was the best in Australia. Simon asked the receptionist for a quiet room. They were ushered into a dimly lit surgery. Kathy sat in the corner with the bird in her lap, gently patting and whispering to it. Simon stroked its soft grey head.

Kathy looked up to Simon to mutter, 'She smells so fresh, just like the ocean.'

Simon nodded.

The wail of a cat burst through the door when the vet came into the room.

The shearwater gargled and attempted to stand as the vet stretched its wings and examined its back. The bird struggled to get away by nipping at the vet's prodding fingers.

'That's right, mate, you fight it to the end,' Simon whispered under his breath.

'Yes, it's a fairly severe fracture of the wing.' The vet shook his head.

'Can it be reset?' asked Kathy.

'No, it's in a really awkward spot.' The vet turned to Simon. 'I'll contact the Department of Conservation tomorrow to see what can be done. I just thought I'd caution you, though: the department's overwhelmed by hundreds of injured birds this time of year. It must have got caught in that storm we had last night.' He placed the struggling bird into a wooden crate. 'We'll probably have to put it down.'

They silently walked out of the surgery.

'What do you want to do now?' Simon opened the door to the car

'I don't know,' murmured Kathy.

'Do you want to go and see the whales?'

'OK. I don't feel like going back to town just yet.'

Simon started the car and followed a series of small blue signs pointing the way to the whale nursery.

Kathy tasted the salt on her lips as she walked up the wooden steps towards the viewing platform. She saw Simon turn red while the sun flared on the horizon. A grey leviathan tail suddenly burst out of the water. Kathy noticed children running and squealing with delight in the shallows below. A mother swung her little girl's feet through the foam.

Simon lit up a cigarette and stared at his feet. 'Do you think we did the right thing?' He slowly rubbed his eyes.

'I don't know, Simon. Probably not…at least it's being cared for. I shudder to think of it dying out in the cold ocean.' Kathy flicked her straw-coloured hair off her cheeks.

Simon watched the mother whale circle her calf. He reflected back to the night his grandfather died and remembered asking the nurse for more morphine to ease the old man's pain. He pictured the way his grandfather's face turned white and bloated like a full moon as his life ebbed away.

'I'll ring them tomorrow. Christ, I hope the poor thing pulls through… Do you want to go for a drink at the Caledonian or something?'

Simon blew smoke up into the air. The beach faded into grey.

'What do you think of the idea of us having a child, Simon?'

Simon stared out into the encroaching night sky. A hole had expanded in his soul ever since the death of his grandfather. It haunted all of his lyrics. It grew now as he recalled the shearwater struggling in the vet's arms. He'd tried to wash this empty feeling away with alcohol, but it refused to go. The rhythm of his guitar used to take his spirit away to some form of heaven. Now, he just seemed to drift through endless nights on a smoke filled stage that reeked of stale piss. Maybe a child would fill the hole, Simon thought. Sea air blew down the front of his collar; his teeth started to chatter. He threw his cigarette away. They got into the car and hugged.

'Well?' she asked.

'I'd probably have to get myself a dreary job, build a nest egg. It would be worthwhile, though, as long as I knew one of us was going to stay home and look after the little one. I could still try to write. So long as you're sure about it, Kath.'

She stared at the canoe moon sailing through white clouds. 'I remember a night years ago in Mallacoota,' she said. 'We were camping. Do you remember? We sat talking by the river, watching the sun go down. I remember you opened up, told me things about yourself that I'd never heard from any other guy before. As you told me things, I kept saying to myself, yeah, yeah, you're spot on. It was like I was having a conversation with my closest friend, yet we'd only known each other for a few months. I still feel that way now, Simon. You're the closest thing to me on this planet. So yeah, I'm sure about it.'

Simon started the engine. The new moon dissolved into the ocean. A bird called from somewhere in the night. The headlights of their car shrank into pinheads before disappearing along the black coast road.

Venture Boys

1999

Joe's coming back to town. Now, there's a boy who knew how to beat the nine-to-five. He's been gone for twelve years, trying his luck in London with his painting. I can picture him now, leaning back on a divan, smoking, explaining his love of Salvador Dali to an enthralled bunch of hangers on. He wants to have lunch with me. Me, of all people! Fat, bald, old public servant me.

I put on my sunnies. The Dandenongs float like a blue peninsula over the morning mist. I'm flying to Ringwood. The sun glides like a white phosphorite ball behind the train. I wish I was still in bed with my baby boy. I love to hear his quick breath. Kathy, my better half, has a long hauling breath like the sea. Rory pants like a puppy. Your daddy's off to earn an honest crust. Are your summer blue eyes open yet? They placed you in my arms minutes after they took you out of your mother's belly. Your eyes said 'I know you.' I saw my dead grandparents in your face, Rory. I drank and wrote about your birth later on that night through tears.

Joseph, my teenage friend. We were the first two at school to get our ears pierced. My dad threatened to thrash me if I got an earring. The doctor pierced Joe's earlobe no worries. When the needle snapped in mine, Joe fainted. My dad threatened to wire me up that night when I was asleep. Two weeks later, when my earring came out. I didn't know how to put it back in. Dad helped me.

Over the murky Yarra we go. Fog curls and dissolves above the river. Grey buildings loom in the yellow smog. Poor Dad; that night he caught me wearing black mascara. Joe and I used to follow Split Enz everywhere around Melbourne after they stepped off the boat from

New Zealand. We loved to put make-up on each other so that we would look like the singers Tim Finn and Phil Judd. We used to paint each other's face in the men's toilet at the Dallas Brooks Hall.

An old hippy staggered into the toilets once, and saw us putting our make-up on each other in front of the mirror. He stared through his red dilated eyes and muttered, 'I don't believe this, man. This isn't reality.'

Here were these two sixteen-year-old boys. I had long red hair down to my bum. Joe had long black hair flowing past his backside. Joe had taken his tiny brush out of his make-up bag and was painting my eyelids. We both had huge diamond patterns painted around our eyes.

'I'm very much afraid this is reality, mate,' declared Joe to the stunned old hippie.

Spencer Street Station; the walking dead shuffle past the ticket machines. I turn my Walkman up, David Bowie's song 'Joe the Lion' blares through my eardrums. There's that busker with the beautiful voice. He's a young fella with long hair and beard. We always give each other a big smile. I throw him some money. Clink. Hello, fellow soul.

1975

'Tim! Phil! Tim! Phil!' We shout with high-pitched voices before Split Enz come on stage. We rock all night. Joe and I sing all the way home on the last Bulleen bus. My dad says something smart to me as I jump into the shower, but I don't give a rats. Images of strobe lights, clown like costumes, mad haircuts, guitars and pianos dance around my young mind.

'Are you all right ,Simon?' my boss, Mr Victa, asked me the next day.

'Yeah, no worries.' I reply as I notice this weird look in his eyes.

'Your eyes are black. Have you been in a blue?'

'Nah.'

'You been crook?'

'No. I'm fine, thanks.' I run off to the toilet and splash water over what's left of the mascara.

Joe comes in, cacking himself silly, clutching a newspaper. 'Have you seen this, Simon?' Joe throws the paper down in front of me.

'What is it?' I stare into the mirror.

'It's an interview with Tim Finn about last night's concert. I've got some make-up remover for that, by the way.'

'Jesus Harry Percival, Joe. I can't get this bloody stuff off. Could you read it out to us?' I rub my eyes to buggery.

'"We noticed our relationship with the Melbourne audience is changing, we actually heard young girls calling out our names before we came on. That's never happened before," stated Tim Finn.'

'You're bloody well kidding. What a classic!'

'No, it's here in black and white. Come here, you silly bugger I'll get it off for you.' Joe washed my eyes then scrubbed away with a paper towel.

'What if the boss comes in?'

'Who gives a rodent's posterior? Now hold still. will you?'

1999

'Remember. Conway. I want you to sign your individual contract today,' ordered my boss Mike Thompson.

'We can be heroes just for one day,' shouts David Bowie into my headphones. I turn the volume down. 'I'll think about it,' I reply.

'It's not a matter of thinking about it, but signing it!'

Stick it right up yours, Thompson. Why should I sign a contract just to keep working in this dump? We never had to sign any contract under the previous government. Mike Thompson has assured us peasants that we can negotiate with management on a level playing field. Negotiations! Pah! More like a killing field. What hope does a lone individual have against management with all their resources? When some of us attempted to negotiate a collective agreement, Mike Thompson said he wouldn't deal with a 'pack of Labor cunts'.

'Heroes' still rings in my ears as I turn my computer on. Great lyrics. I wrote stories and poems when I was a teenager. When I showed them to Joe, he loved them. I used to write in bed in that in-between time before sleep. Joe said we should put my poems to music and form a band. Whenever a favourite song came on the transistor radio under my pillow, I used to picture Joe as the lead singer and me as the lead guitarist. I still do. There I am in my fantasy, posturing with a full crop of hair and a skinny body. Go Joe and I…I still manage to write now and then when my heart's raw. I open my first file for the day and wonder what Joe looks like now.

1975

'I remember the first time I heard David Bowie's "Starman",' Joseph said. 'I was travelling in the back seat of my dad's Valiant. He was taking the family for our first ride up the Tullamarine freeway not long after it had opened. I was leaning back, listening to the trannie, looking up at all the neon lights flashing by, when "Starman" came on. By the time the song had finished, I was praying to the stars for a spaceship to come and take me away from it all.'

'You might get taken away one day, Joe,' I said one Friday night a few weeks later. We'd just finished a night's work at Venture. 'I've just read this amazing book my uncle lent me which says there's a civilisation below the surface of the planet called Derros. They come up to the surface in UFOs and kidnap people in remote areas. They want to learn all they can about us, before they enslave us. They keep us like exhibits in a zoo. They sometimes put a naked man in with a naked woman in a specially heated cell, to see how we reproduce.'

'Wow! Nice work when you can get it. Ciggie?' asked Joseph.

'Ta.'

'What flavour? I've rolled lemon, pineapple, banana, lime…or strawberry.'

'I'll have strawberry this time, thanks.'

We lit our cigarettes and blow smoke up into the night sky; the Southern Cross shimmered like a silver kite.

'I wish you hadn't told me that,' Joe said. 'You know I have to cross Koonung Creek to get home, don't you? C'mon! Derros!' My mate shouted to the full moon as he took off for home. 'See you tomorrow, Simon, I hope.'

I heard his faraway laugh as his silhouette dissolved into the darkness.

Next morning at Venture, we set up an outdoor display of bikes.

'You know I stood on something as I crossed the creek. It reared up and grabbed my ankle. I thought it was a Derro, trying to drag me down to Derro land. I bloody ran all the way home. I tried to sleep. But something fell onto the chair at the bottom of my bed. It was hooded.'

'Jesus Harry, according to my uncle's book, Derros wear hoods, Joe!'

'Well, I bloody well had a staring competition. I was paralysed with fear for ages until I summoned up enough courage to flick the light on and discover I was having a staring match with my jumper. I was going to tell you off this morning, but I had this amazing dream. Do Derro women have long blonde hair?'

'Yeah, they do. Why do you ask?'

'I dreamt of hundreds of fair women bathing in a river. They eventually discarded their long light blue gowns then performed this slow water ballet to this amazing ethereal music completely starkers. Before I knew it, I was a fish nibbling at their ankles, then all the way up their long legs to heaven. God, it was wonderful. So thank you, Simon. Without you, I don't think I would have experienced such a fabulous dream.'

'God! Why can't I have a dream like that?' I cursed to myself.

'Hey, youse two, stop bullshitting to each other and start selling bikes, will ya!' shouted Mr Victa.

He's not a bad old codger. Sometimes he loves to beep his car horn and give us the two-fingered salute when he sees us at the milk bar sipping our thick shakes after work. Joe and I always laugh and salute him back. He once told us some customers complained about the way we carried naked mannequins from one floor to another. We told him the only way you could carry the awkward bloody things was to grip them firmly on the crutch and chest.

Joe loves to kneel down on top of the wooden lay-by shelves and dangle naked dummy legs over the side. As I come into the lay-by department, I hear this enticing voice whispering, 'Simon, oh Simon, come up here, big boy, and I'll show you a good time.'

I look up to the top of the shelves to spy what looks like Joe stroking his long naked legs. I wet myself silly laughing.

Mr Victa sometimes takes a Venture girl out to his car on Friday nights. Joe stuck his head out of the storeroom door one night to see our boss pashing some poor unfortunate girl. My mate motioned to me to stick my head around the outside door with him. I did and saw Mr Victa going at it to such an extent I was afraid he'd lose his false teeth. We went back inside and grabbed a dummy head each. Suddenly four heads peer around the door at Mr Victa. He's got his right arm wrapped around a Venture girl's head and waves with his left arm for us to go away.

When Joe and I and our two mates insist on watching the show, he jumps out of the car and storms up to us shouting, 'Right, you two blokes are gone! Scarfo, Conway, I recognised you, but who were those other two bastards?'

1999

'God, I miss you both. How's Rory?' I ask.

'He's having his morning nap,' Kathy says on the other side of the line.

'I might see if I can get more family leave.'

'You don't want to use it all up yet, Simon. Remember your plans.'

'I know, I know, but I want to be home with you guys again. I've got more out of my month home with you and Rory than I'll ever get out of a lifetime of work.'

'It's your call, Simon. How's your morning been?'

'Faye, Libby, Anne, Sophie, Linda…they've all been wonderful. They've asked a million questions about you and Rory. They all send their love.'

'What about Bill?'

'What about Bill? He's said nothing, like all the other boring male farts in this office. One dickhead manager came up to me and said all I talk about is babies and it's time to focus on work. I told him that Rory's the best thing that's ever happened to me.'

'Have they said anything about signing the contract?'

'As soon as I came in. You know practically everybody else has signed one. Thompson's hinted that he'll sack me if I don't. So much for us living in a free country. Stupid Liberals! Anyway, I'm gonna see if I can get more time off from this dump.'

'I'd better go, sweetie. Rory's just woken up. Have a good lunch with Joseph.'

1975

It's midday in December. We sit on top of a hill behind our school, sketching an old man gum tree. Joe's teaching me how to make my drawing of the tree trunk circular. We love to talk about the Renaissance and how ancient knowledge returned to Italy after scholars, priests and painters fled from the fallen empire of Byzantium. How Europe flourished again, after a thousand years of darkness. Joe believes we're going through another Dark Age now they've sacked Gough.

'Australians are so sado-masochistic, Simon. Hold your pencil like this. Along comes a great man like Whitlam. He appeals to our better nature, makes you feel good about being an Australian. Yes, that's it. See, your trunk is starting to appear round now. We produce great writers, brilliant painters, unique ideas and fabulous movies. Then the small-minded voter comes along and says, "Oh no, we've gone too far." That's it, Simon, you've got it. See, the trunk doesn't look like a cardboard cut-out any more. It's time to lower our expectations. Here we are, Mr Fraser, we're exposing our buttocks. We must be punished, it's time for a serious thrashing. God, in Europe, there'd be a revolution against what those Liberal slimebags have done. Don't forget when you paint your shadow it has to be the opposite colour to the tree.'

'What colour do you recommend, Joey,' I asked.

'A good strong purple. Nothing like a good strong purple.'

'Ta.'

'In this Dark Age, you, I and others are sowing the seeds. You've got to continue with your writing, I'm determined to keep my painting going. It's important not to be overwhelmed by the deadheads of this world, Simon. Australia's a young country. If we persist with our dreams, we'll be remembered. That's it, Simon. What a great tree you've just created! I mean, we Europeans have pulled down all the trees. Our decaying monuments dominate the land. Here…there's hundreds of miles of wilderness, no sign of man for as far as you can see. Huge areas that man hasn't stuffed up yet. Areas that we've yet to give expression to. You Australians…'

'Will you stop it with this "you Australians" bullshit, for Christ's sake. You were born in Fitzroy,' I lectured.

'You Australians always remind me that I'm a wog.'

'You're not just a wog, Scarfo, you're a fucking poofta as well. If you don't shut the fuck up, I'll come over there and make you shut up,' shouted our class dickhead Leigh Nesbit.

'You can attempt to punch me witless, but it won't change my opinion of you,' replied Joe.

'Get stuffed, Nesbit! There, what do you reckon Joe? Is that a gum tree, or is that a gum tree?' I boasted.

'It's a decent painting now, Simon… Although you should make your purple a bit deeper,' said Joe. 'Sorry, Simon…you know I'm such a fuss bum.'

'That's all right, Joe, I know.'

I looked up from my sketch. I'll never forget the hurt look on Joe's face that hot summer's day. He'd been regularly accused of being a poof by the bandaged-knuckle brigade of our school.

1999

It's nearly noon. Rory's due for his bottle. I'd normally be feeding him by now. Are you doing your little medley, Rory? Kathy reckons you've learnt how to sing by listening to the magpies at dawn. One thing I want to teach him when he gets older is never be afraid of sticking out from the herd. Time to see Joe.

God, the sunlight makes you squint. The old sluggish Yarra has turned silver. There he is. I'd recognise that skinny frame anywhere.

'Hello,' said Joe with an impeccable British accent.

'Joey?'

'Simon, you look terrible. How are you?'

We hugged each other.

'You probably heard we had the little fella two months ago. Things have been pretty blurry ever since. How are you, you wonderful bugger?'

'I'm fabulous. Congratulations on the little man. The old Simon is a father! Unbelievable! Is everything OK now?'

'We're over the worst of it. Thank God. Kathy is still a bit tender with all the stitches and stuff. Little Rory's is going to need a few more operations. But the little sweetie should be OK.'

'How does it feel to be a father?'

'God…I feel like Kathy and I have been shoved into another existence and the door has been shut firmly behind us. My past has gone forever. I feel uncertain yet…good. Kathy and I haven't had a decent sleep since Rory entered this planet…but the look he gives me, Joe…it's worth it. Enough about me. How are you? How's your painting going. Have you conquered Europe yet?'

'That's on the back-burner for now.'

'So what are you doing with yourself?'

'I've had a series of customer service jobs over the years. I'm a health and fitness instructor now,' said Joe.

'You a health freak! You're not painting at all?'

'Not for a while. You know how it is.'

'I know exactly how it is, Joey.'

'How's your job?'

'We've all been put under huge pressure to sign individual contracts. I can't sign my soul away to the devil… Do you want to grab something to eat and go down to the river, Joe? '

'Yeah! Don't worry, Simon, we had all that bollocks under Thatcher and now she's gone.'

As Joe spoke about what he'd gotten up to in London, I couldn't help reflecting on how he'd ended up as a health and fitness instructor! With his weed of a frame, he couldn't bench press a banana. C'mon, tram, shift yourself from the middle of the road. I park my large behind on the grass. Piss off, seagull, there's a good bird. The sun's biting my sparse scalp. Joe has still got all of his hair. My God, he's got such muscular biceps! We're still working like two Venture Boys after all. Our dreams…have they evaporated like this morning's fog?

'I'd forgotten how objects in the sky over here are so big, Simon.' Joe sat down next to me. 'Take the dying moon over there. It's huge. Last night, before I went to sleep, I looked out through my sister's attic window. Jesus, the sky was a silver broth of stars! You never get that in London. I remember we used to go and find a sunny bank by the Yarra on the weekend. We'd chat and stare out at the view. I'd bring a sketchpad along. You'd bring an exercise book,' said Joe.

'Now all we've got in our hands are sandwiches,' I replied.

'Don't be so negative, Simon. I love what I'm doing now. I meet so many interesting people. London is central to everything. Every chance I get I go off to Europe and America. Right now, I'm madly in love with Florida.'

'I'm jealous. God, the farthest I get these days is maybe Airey's inlet,' I said.

'If anyone's jealous around here, it's me… A steady relationship with Kathy for twelve years. My record's six months. You've got a little message in a bottle…a son. Someone who'll remember you and talk about you after you've gone. What's Kathy like?'

'She's the same star sign as you. You'd love her. You'll have to come over and meet her. She loves a good gas bag like we do.'

'Sorry, Simon, but I fly off to Sydney tomorrow, then back home to London after that. Maybe next time,' said Joe.

'Sure, Joey… I'd love to come over. Anyway, I'd better stumble back to the orifice. Take care.'

'Same to you, Simon,' said Joe.

We hugged each other and said goodbye.

To buy a newspaper or not buy a newspaper? UFOs SEEN OVER BASS STRAIT! Methinks not to buy a paper. Who's that smiling below that jogger's hood? God, it's Thompson's right-hand man, the vampire-looking Steve Ferella. I'd recognise his boof head anywhere.

'You're signing that contract today, aren't you?' Steve demanded, jogging up and down on the spot.

'Is this going back to Thompson?' I asked him. Silly question really.

'Yes. Why?'

'Then tell him to shove it as far as it fits!' I walked back towards the train station.

Midway Through Life's Dream

Midway this way of life we're bound upon,
I woke to find myself in a dark wood,
Where the right road was wholly lost and gone.
– Dante, *The Divine Comedy*

On 21 December at midday, Dominic Balento sat down on a log in the shade to get away from everybody else. Through the top of the mountain ashes he saw a grey halo around the sun and promised himself that this was going to be his last birthday celebration.

Barbecue smoke ghosted around the giant trunks of the forest trees. He heard his father Leo scraping the spatula and his mother Cecilia giving endless orders on how best to cook the meat. Through the smoke he made out the figure of his younger sister Marguerite, staring at him while she breastfed her daughter. A car door slammed. Dominic stared at Tom, the son of his friend Julian Tregear, who jumped out of the back seat in his knight's costume. The boy growled as he stuck his sword into the belly of an imaginary dragon.

'G'day, Dom. Happy birthday, old son.' Julian shook Dominic's hand.

'Happy birthday, Dominic.' Jessica Tregear pecked his bearded cheek and handed him a present.

'It's amazing how the two people closest to me on this planet were born on solstice day, you in summer and Jessica in winter.' Julian laughed to himself. 'So how are you going, you old bugger? What did you get for presents?'

'Nothing yet. Besides, who bloody well cares? It's just another day like any other. Christ, I wish people wouldn't make such a bloody fuss!' Dominic glared at Julian.

'C'mon, Dom, open it up!' Jessica's hazel eyes glowed.

'Charge!' shouted Tom as he took his plastic sword from his scabbard and jumped onto the picnic table. The boy circled his blade at the grey clouds above and challenged them to a duel. The clouds retreated. His blue eyes looked down at Dominic and saw the old man from the bank in *Mary Poppins*. Tom hoped his present would cheer him up.

Julian watched Dominic place the unopened present on the log then retreat towards the car park.

'Don't worry, Julian. He's always miserable this time of year. Leave him be. He'll pick up now that you're here.' Marguerite placed her baby over her shoulder and rubbed its back.

Julian half smiled and shook his head. Tom giggled at the baby's burps.

Dominic slouched in the front seat of his car. His yellow-tinged eyes focused on a young magpie scuttling along the ground towards his parents. One adult bird stuck its beak up to warble at the midday sun; the other fed the baby some sausage meat. Dominic thought of how his mother was usually melancholic on his birthday. He was about the same age as Tom when he discovered he had a twin, a stillborn brother. Years later when Dominic became an artist, images of his brother haunted his paintings.

'He needs a part-time job to get a grip on the real world.' Marguerite placed her dozing daughter in a pram. 'When you live like a hermit, your mind wanders. You know, he told me the other day that he can actually feel the earth rotating?'

Julian nodded, thinking of the succession of dead-end jobs he had had over the years. He looked over to Jessica, who was chatting to Leo and Cecilia.

'How is your old man?' Julian crossed his arms over his chest.

'He's all right. I've been trying to tell him that he mightn't have anything wrong. A shadow on the prostate doesn't mean he's going to die. It can be treated.' As Marguerite spoke, Julian noticed that she had her brother's dark eyes. 'He's so much like Dominic!' Marguerite rocked the pram. 'Both of them always assume the worst. Even though the tests showed nothing definite, Dad's convinced his body is riddled with cancer.'

Tom bounded through a flock of rosellas, causing a shrieking red cloud to fly to the top of the forest. Julian stared up at the screaming birds and studied the horn of a new moon fading into the afternoon haze.

'Daddy, I've got to show you a sad tree!' Tom pounced onto his father's lap.

'Sad? What's so sad about it, mate?' Julian leant down to rescue his son's dropped shield.

The boy clung to him like a baby koala. 'It's fallen down, right down into the forest!'

'All right, Tom Tom, maybe after lunch. See, Leo and Cecilia are handing around the plates.'

Leo, clutching his wineglass in one hand and a plate of food in the other, grunted as he slowly sat down next to Julian. 'You know, Julius, you gotta stop drinking the beer. Only crass people drink beer.'

'Crass is my middle name, Leo.' Julian raised his eyebrows.

Leo chuckled. The older man noticed Julian's black boots; they were identical to the boots the men wore in Melbourne when he stepped off the boat in 1949. Those plodding black boots, blue singlets and green army shorts were standard summer wear back then. During the war, his Uncle Caesar sent him letters from a prisoner of war camp in Australia. He wrote of a cloudless, never-ending red landscape. He told stories of Australian troops with their casual green army uniform, sharing cigarettes and alcohol with the inmates. The complete opposite to those slick black-shirted demons who mercilessly patrolled the streets of Rome.

Some of the best conversations Leo ever had were in the factories of North Melbourne. Some Aussies would sit mouth agape when he told them of his life in wartime Italy. How Allied fighters circled the city like hornets then roared as they swooped down to shoot at anything that moved in the surrounding countryside. His fellow workmates would ask questions and listen and yarn; unlike his tertiary-educated compatriots in Rome, who loved to shout over each other about their latest theory.

Man ferns embraced the sun while Leo and Julian talked, drank and laughed into the afternoon.

Dominic came back along the trail. Cecilia stared at her son's paint-spattered clogs, shaking her head to mutter, '*Dio mio,* Pino. *Come sei combinato*!

'Ma, be quiet, will you,' Marguerite hissed.

Leo held up his glass and smiled at the yellow amoeba of sunlight dancing in the middle of his red wine. Jessica gently ran her fingers through her son's thick mop of blond hair while he dreamt in her lap.

'You know my shrink is a practising Christian.' Dominic gave a disgusted look at the food and sat down.

'Fair dinkum?' Julian squinted at his friend.

'Despite his clinical training, he believes there's life after death.'

Leo stood up and walked towards his daughter. Marguerite responded to his moaning, but still had one ear turned to her brother's conversation.

'Well then, I'm sure you'd have a lot to talk about!' Julian rubbed his tired eyes. Tom had woken up at five in the morning.

'He believes there is another existence out there...' Dominic gestured to the sky, 'which operates irrespective of how we think or act. An existence we return to when we die. Do you believe in an afterlife, Julian?'

'I've got some sort of spirituality, but not as it's taught by the fanatics of this world. Even if I could believe in life after death, I think that you would no longer exist as before. Don't most religions teach that once you snuff it, you become a part of a god in some state of amazing grace without the dangly bits of your body. Even if the god, who is always a male by the way, decides to send you back as a frog or something, from what I've heard you return with no memory of any previous life, so you as an individual are wiped out anyway.'

'I'm terrified by the idea that once you die, there's nothing left!' Dominic shouted. 'I mean, here I am at forty-one. Twenty years ago, you and I were as drunk as skunks dancing all night celebrating my twenty- first. Twenty years have zoomed by. Before we know it, twenty years will zoom by again and we'll be old bloody men. Leo and Cecilia won't be here any more. It'll be our generation's turn to stare down into the valley. I mean, here am I midway through my life and what have I done? Tell me, what have I done?'

'Well, your folks' house is stacked with your paintings for starters.'

'Yeah, but that's not enough. I'm terrified of stinking death, the finality of it all, rotting away beneath six feet of clay, me being just snuffed out. Christ, it's terrifying!'

'Maybe you're not snuffed out,' Julian replied. 'When my Granddad Thomas died, I was there with him. He kept saying that he just wanted to sleep. His children kept waking him up, but he finally went with my mother stroking his brow. I was ripped to shreds standing by his bed, but…I felt, it's hard to put into words, I felt as if something chemical took place between him and me…some of him flowed into me. Call it what you will, his soul maybe, I don't know, but I do know something from Granddad settled into me.'

'It probably did.' Marguerite rocked her baby who gurgled and played with her mother's gold necklace.

They were silent for a while then Tom woke up. 'Mummy, I dreamed I was a mermaid like Ariel, and I swam and swam as far as I could out into the sea until the water was green.' The yawning boy stretched his arms and stared up at his mother.

Jessica traced her fingers along Tom's forehead and smiled. Cecilia flicked flies out of the sky with her tea towel.

'You know, women don't think the same way about death as we do, Tregear.' Dominic lowered his voice.

'That's because they're too bloody busy.' Julian raised his hand. 'Huh?'

'Look around you. Cecilia's doing the cleaning up and constantly chatting to Leo to distract him from his worry. Marguerite is always keeping an eye on you. She once complained to me that she never has the luxury of a good conversation because she's always squeezed between the demands of you and your old man! Jessica has spent most of the afternoon reassuring Leo that everything's going to be all right. They're immersed in the more important things, while we talk rubbish on the edge of life. They're the sun, we're planets revolving around them, obsessed by our own petty little concerns. Anyway, mate, the little one is asking Jessica for a look around the forest. Time for a walk, eh?'

'I'll stay here.' Dominic stared down at a dying bee.

Sunlight trickled through the giant trunks to illuminate the ferns. The mountain ashes pumped eucalyptus scents up into the gathering north wind. Tom held his father's hand and chatted to him about Puffing Billy. Jessica was behind them talking to Marguerite.

'I was driving somewhere on a winding road on the outskirts of town. As I came round a sharp bend of the road, I saw a truck in the same lane as me. There was no sound as we collided, but I felt the impact. There was a moment where I didn't see anything…then I opened my eyes. The car was buckled around me. I was completely immobile.'

'You didn't feel anything?' Marguerite pushed the pram uphill.

'I felt no pain. The only things I could see were trees.' Jessica stared at the path in front of them.

'What sort of trees?' Marguerite crinkled her brow.

'Like the ones around us now. I saw them midway up. I couldn't see the base, or the tops, just the middle branches. I felt a strange feeling of ease, and at the same time relief and freedom. There was a sense that I was dead, but it didn't bother me in the slightest.'

Tom turned his head over his shoulder to notice his mother's far away eyes.

'I had a kind of "Oh well" feeling. It was as if a whole different consciousness had taken over me. There was just this wonderful feeling of indifference, as if the past wasn't worth being sentimental or mournful about – there was no future to worry about or contemplate. I was in a state of "right now". I felt no hatred, nor love, nor sense of being hard done by or desire to get back to where I was. I just was. There was a thought – well, not a thought as such because I didn't feel myself thinking anything either – but there was this feeling all the time of "God, this is nice". My body felt fluid. I felt a strange sense of enlightenment like "so this is what it's really about" as if I suddenly understood something along the lines of there being no notion of good or evil or right or wrong. Because it's not necessary, it's not needed. It doesn't matter, nothing matters, it never has and it never will. And I felt this wonderful sense of freedom or release. Nothing bothered me any more. But then I began to hear sounds again, like the way you hear sounds when you're under the water, dull, slow clunking sounds. And I stopped seeing trees and instead I saw the head of a man. He was trying to get me out of the car, pulling away the wreckage. And I was disappointed that he was doing it – I suddenly began to feel responsible for myself again and what was happening to me and I guess I felt that I was alive after all…'

'When was this?' Marguerite halted the pram.

'Last winter, near my birthday. ' Jessica stopped then walked on.

Julian remembered; he had lain next to her on the bed that morning, stroking her long fair hair as she recalled her dream. He sympathised with her feeling of remoteness that day.

Clank, clank, clank, went the steady rhythm of Leo's walking stick. The old man sweated as he sucked the forest's breath deep into his lungs. Cecilia shuffled beside him with the tea towel now sitting on top of her head. Moss carpeted the limbs of blackwood trees.

Leo ruffled the downy hair of his dozing granddaughter then muttered to Julian, 'You know, when I first came up here, I'd always see a lyrebird. I wonder if she'll see any when she gets older? Stupid bloody man!'

'There's another one,' yelled Tom.'Look at it, poor sad tree. Look, Mummy.' The boy dragged Jessica away from Marguerite.

Julian approached the huge trunk sprawled across the forest floor.

Tom whispered to Jessica, 'It's dead. Look, he's fallen down on his side, Mummy.'

'No, it's not, darling. He's just an old tree having a nap.' Jessica smiled.

Beautiful old fella, Julian thought to himself while he patted the upturned roots.

'Tomaso, Tomaso!' Cecilia's muffled voice sang out from a hollow in the tree. '*Veni qui, guarda!*'

'Go on, Tommy, have a look. Nothing will happen to you, I promise. The tree's our mate.' Julian took his son's hand.

Cecilia pulled her head from out of the trunk to beckon Tom to follow her. The boy wearily approached. Cecilia crouched back into the tree and whispered, 'Tomaso, *quarda, un alberello*'

Thomas peered into a dark hollow, to see a sapling sprouting from the inside of the dead mountain ash.

Dominic opened up his present that night. It was a framed painting Tom had done of a clown with a beaming smile on his face. As the artist went into his studio and sketched, he felt the earth tilting towards the sun as it sped through the dust sprinkled emptiness of space.

A year later when Julian booked their favourite Italian restaurant to celebrate Dominic's forty-second, the birthday boy pulled out at the last minute. The Balentos and Tregears still managed to have a good time. With a belly full of wine and pizza, Julian dozed in front of his TV until the shrill noise of the phone startled him out of his blissful state. Yet once more, up until midnight, he managed to help talk Dominic out of his blues.

'For how much longer?' he started asking himself as heard his dreaming wife call through the dark.

Hello Goodbye

Tim could do a whole range of brum, brum sounds long before he learnt to talk. He loves anything to do with engines. Once when he was playing with his Matchbox cars on the floor, our friend Margaret exclaimed, 'Oh, listen to him, he's even changing gears.'

Tim heard an engine down the street while I read to him. We decide to go out and investigate after his last story.

'I reckon it could be a big lawnmower or a digger. What do you reckon, mate?' I ambled down the street holding Tim's hand while he nursed his furry possum puppet to his chest. Walking slowly was one of the first lessons my son taught me now I was no longer part of the rat race.

'Hmm…' Tim's blue eyes were lost in thought. 'I reckon it could be that bobcat we saw the other day.' He stopped at a waxy green bush on the corner and knelt down to study some soldier beetles. 'Dad, why are they stuck together like that?' Tim placed his hand on the footpath and encouraged two enjoined beetles on to his little fingers.

'I'm not sure, mate. Maybe they're making babies like you saw in your dinosaur video.' Another lesson Tim had taught me: be open about things. This had taken some time, because I'd spent a decade in a crowded office where in order to survive the last thing you did was reveal your innermost thoughts.

Tim and I watched the little black and red beetles go about their business. I used to fly around this corner every morning to catch the train into the city. Some of the people I worked with laughed when I said I was going on family leave to stay home and look after my son.

One colleague stated, 'I knew a bloke down the road who did that and he ended up turning into an alcoholic.'

My director tittered, 'You'll be ringing up in a few weeks time begging me to come back.'

Well, she may be a director of work but she's a lousy observer of life, because here I am two years later still looking after my little man.

The engine sound whirred as we crossed the road and made our way to the railway station. Tim jumped up and down and pointed to the other side of the track at an orange bobcat preparing the ground for a footpath. I shook my head and smiled back at him. We sat down on a platform seat to chat about the bobcat. The driver smiled and waved when he saw us. Tim and I laughed and waved back. The little boy in the man, who drives big machines, surfaces when he notices a child watching him. He always gets a happy gleam in his eye.

School kids trickled on to the platform across the other side. I stared up at the swollen grey clouds sailing towards the Dandenongs and took a deep breath.

Winter's on her way. You pay more attention to Mother Nature when you're away from work. One of my favourite pastimes these days is making a fire in our hearth, grabbing a drink and having Tim on my lap. We watch the flames and he tells me of worlds where dragons blow mists and spit red stars up at the sky. My son claps and dances whenever I tell him I'm going to make a fire.

A tall skinny man with long grey hair and a shaggy silver beard marched towards us. As he got closer, I noticed he had a huge glob of snot hanging down from his nostril to his chin. His wrinkled face looked wild. Don't sit down next to me, I said under my breath. But he did and pulled a packet of cigarettes out of the breast pocket of his crumpled brown suit top.

'The next bloody train's an express, which means it's not gonna stop at my station! I live in Auburn. Hardly any train stops there these days!' He lit up a cigarette and shot me an angry look.

Christ, what do I say back to this bloke? I shrugged.

'Uh oh!' Tim jumped off the seat and pointed to a teenager who'd jumped down on to the rails to retrieve his yellow footy. 'He shouldn't do that, should he, Dad?' Tim shook his head.

'No, mate. It's dangerous.' I scratched my beard.

'He doesn't miss a trick, does he?' The man smiled and nodded towards Tim.

'He's an intelligent little monkey, all right.' I replied, relieved that the ice had been broken.

'How old is he?' The man tapped his ash on to the ground.

'Six months!' Tim declared as he climbed back next to me.

'You're four, mate, remember?' I chuckled and leant towards him to count four on my fingers.

My son followed with his eyes and lips.

The sign said the Flinders Street train was due in fifteen minutes.

Tim smiled shyly as he stretched over my lap and held his possum up to the man.

'I was wondering what that was. I thought it was a flaming cat.' The man raised his eyebrows and roared out a laugh.

Tim responded with a similar laugh then made a series of guttural possum sounds. Some of the school kids on the other side appeared puzzled by the man's booming laughter.

'Why's he got a possum? Most kid's have teddies.' The man wiped his moist eyes.

'Tim loves possums. We've got a family that visits us every night to knock off our food scraps. He loves hand-feeding them.'

'I feed them Toblerone chocolate in Fitzroy Gardens. Some of the little buggers run right up to me and rip it right out of my hand. Do you guys live around here?' He butted out his cigarette and lit another. He spent more time holding them in a claw-like grip rather than smoking them.

'Just round the corner in Viviani Crescent.'

'I've spent the day with my sister… She lives in Great Ryrie. I can't get over your little man. The possum sounds he makes are spot on. He's smart, all right. That takes lots of observation.'

'When they first put him in my arms, he stared right through me. He'd only been on this planet for a few seconds but he knew me already. The nurses used to tell me that while all the other babies cried or slept in the hospital, Tim was quiet and watched everything going on around him.' I fended Tim off from attacking my face with his possum.

'That's a bit rough, isn't it?' The man grinned and took a deep drag on his cigarette. 'I'm a paranoid schizophrenic on the pension. I barely get enough money to eat and pay the rent. It's even harder to do the simple things of life like having a few beers with my mates now and then. My sister nagged me all bloody day about going on a budget, but I find something like that bloody impractical.'

'I reckon a budget's the first nail in the coffin.' I recalled how my wife had recently suggested the same thing and I told her I just couldn't think that way.

The man's grey eyes widened.

The sign said the Flinders Street train was due in ten minutes.

'The rich are getting richer. Everyone's out for themselves these days. All everyone seems to care about is money. What about ethics, eh? It's pathetic they way people display their material possessions to each other. One of the first things you're supposed to learn as a kid is not show off.' He snorted as he pulled a dirty hanky out of his tracksuit pants to wipe away the snot. Another blob soon dripped down his whiskers.

'I've never had a job, you know.' He gazed down at his sandals.

'That's all right. You're not missing much. Most jobs are pretty boring anyway. I've got more out of life by staying home and looking after Tim than I'll ever get from years of work.'

'Take a look at those kids over there. They're all brimming with energy and life. Look at them laughing, chatting and playing games with each other. Yet once they enter the workforce they shuffle around the streets like zombies. All their joy's gone. Everywhere I go, I see people walking around with miserable looks on their faces. They spend all day working for a boss and doing things they really don't want to do.' The man threw his half-smoked cigarette on to the track and lit another.

'You're not wrong. I'm so glad to be away from all that garbage.' Tim jumped on to my lap and I rubbed his back.

The platform opposite us was now jammed packed with school kids. The bobcat driver turned his engine off and we waved goodbye to each other as he leapt into his van.

The man stood up to take another look at the sign. 'God, ten minutes is too bloody long to wait for a bloody train. Eeverything in life is stacked against me, that's why I'm a paranoid schizophrenic.' He sat down and laughed again.

I found this man's thunderous laughter infectious and couldn't help warming to him. I asked him his name.

'Frank.'

'G'day, Frank. I'm Keith and this is Tim.' I shook his hand and asked Tim to say hello.

'Hello. Uh oh! He shouldn't do that, should he, Dad?' Tim pointed to the teenager who now stood on the roof of the train station rescuing his yellow footy.

'Yep, you're right, mate.'

The teenager kicked his ball down to his friends.

'He's a big kinder boy now, Frank.'

Tim's eyes lit up.

'My mother never sent me to kinder. She said they were "enclaves of socialism".'

'Ah well…there's nothing wrong with an enclave of socialism, is there, Tim? The world needs more of them.'

My son beamed as Frank and I laughed.

'My mum was a Mick and she raised me as a Catholic. As a little boy, I was forced to think about some pretty heavy things, I tell you. That's why I probably ended up being a paranoid schizophrenic.'

'I'm a half-caste. My mum's a Catholic, my dad's a heathen. She wanted to raise me as a Mick but Dad put his foot down.'

'That was probably a good thing. My personality and morality were paralysed by the church. As a kid, I was shit-scared by the idea of God up in the sky watching over everything I did.' Frank sniffed and pulled out his hanky again. He threw his cigarette on to the tracks then lit up another.

The smoke wafted over us.

A bright-eyed Tim poked his finger into it and sang, 'Whew! Whew! Whew!'

Frank and I laughed when Tim said there was a bellbird down the track smoking a cigarette. The kids directly across from us raised their frowning heads to stare at Frank.

The sign said the Flinders Street train was due in five minutes.

'Where are you guys headed for?' Frank cradled another cigarette.

'We're going home to cook tea and listen to the Beatles. Tim loves getting out his ukulele and strumming along to their music.'

'Two of them are dead now.' Frank sighed. 'God, how I loved the Beatles. Their music was so positive and uplifting! Those were the days when giants walked amongst us.'

'What other sort of music do you like, Tim?' I took a water bottle out of my coat pocket and offered it to him.

'The Moody Blues.' Tim held his bottle up like a trumpet player and gulped.

'The Moody Blues!' Frank's face flushed. 'I love the Moody Blues. I'm an old hippie. I smoked too much dope and that's why I ended up being a paranoid schizophrenic too.'

'I love "Nights in White Satin" and "Mull of Kintyre",' Tim gasped after draining his bottle.

'What other songs do you love, mate?' I patted his head.

'"Hello Goodbye" and "Get Back".' Tim flicked my hand away.

'I bloody love those songs too.'

Frank sang "Hello Goodbye" to a grinning Tim. I sang along with him.

The sign said the Flinders Strrrt train was due in one minute.

Frank stared at a young mother who walked by pushing a pram. He stomped on his cigarette and lit up another. 'This world's got a sick sense of priorities. We idolise rich idiots. Anyone can be a successful rich idiot. All you have to do is behave like a spoilt brat and demand that everything goes your way. Yet that woman over there is doing the most important job in the world. A job that's overlooked and taken for granted. Time and time again a mother sacrifices herself for her child that takes a lot of courage. Women are stronger than men.'

Frank held his cigarette on his lap like he was burning a stick of incense. There were so many questions I wanted to ask, but the city train suddenly zoomed below the bridge towards us.

'We'll probably never meet again.' Frank stood and ruffled Tim's hair. 'It's been wonderful meeting you, little fella.'

'Goodbye, mate. Take good care of yourself.' I shook his hand.

As Frank slowly made his way to the carriage, he turned back to stare at Tim waving goodbye with his possum.

I felt sad watching Frank's train disappear down the line. I pictured him sitting in the carriage with snot trickling down his beard, getting disgusted looks from other passengers. I wish I there to tell them to mind their own bloody business! I recalled the joyful way Frank responded to Tim and saw him in the pub laughing away with his mates. Poor old Frank, he was probably one of the sanest persons I'd ever met. Yet he was an outsider.

The Belgrave train arrived to pick up the school kids.

I was annoyed with myself over the judgement I first made when Frank stormed towards us. Well, Tim had taught me another lesson: be generous to strangers. I shivered as I watched the Dandenongs dissolve below the rain clouds. The sky changes regardless of how we act. I held my son's warm hand and made a detour to the bottle shop on our way back home to the Beatles.

The Magpies

In the middle of the night, Melanie listened to the magpies. She'd entered the final trimester of her pregnancy; it felt like someone was doing gymnastics inside her. Melanie smiled as she rubbed her swollen belly and caressed the little one's head.

The magpies warbled through to the early hours of the morning. They were her companions when she drifted between sleep and dreams. Melanie's family believed that magpies were the souls of dead relatives. When they cocked their heads to the side and listened as she spoke, she knew it was true.

The baby kicked away. Melanie reflected on how the birds had become more noticeable now she was off work. During the middle of the day, she'd hear them stomping on the roof like pterodactyls or notice a little black and white silhouette through the frosted window in the front entranceway. Melanie would step out the front door to see a magpie perched on the wooden rail of her porch and three others in the driveway. When she'd break bread and feed, she was convinced she was being visited by her dead grandparents.

Blaise Trezise, the last of her grandparents, had died barely a year ago. Melanie's boyfriend, Leigh, couldn't handle her grief and left her. When her breasts got sore and her stomach swelled, the doctor said it was just a build-up of fluid. It was too late to do anything about it when she discovered she was pregnant. Melanie had a slim frame so she could cover things up for a while. She tried to contact Leigh but discovered he'd flown off overseas. When she summoned up the courage to tell her parents, her father's chin sank to his chest. Melanie was told they'd help her any way they could. Her father, Arthur, gave her something towards the rent and bills for Melanie's house in the foothills of the Dandenongs. Melanie's mother, Lilla, knitted a Collingwood guernsey and bed rug.

Melanie worshipped her granddad. She had a black and white picture of him on her bedside cabinet: Blaise is proudly displaying his Collingwood scarf with a grin from ear to ear at the packed Melbourne Cricket Ground after the Magpies won the 1958 grand final. He often took her to the footy. The old man would get chatty as he built a tower of empty beer cans on the boundary line fence behind the goal posts. He'd told her how his mining father William, came out to Ballarat from Cornwall during the gold rush. William Trezise decided to barrack for Collingwood because the football team's black and white colours matched the Cornish flag.

William told his son that although he didn't strike it rich on his claim, he was fortunate enough to see the original inhabitants of this land perform a corroboree. He noticed how during the ceremony the young men kicked a ball made out of rolled-up possum skin to each other. The man who flew highest to catch the ball got the loudest cheer from his tribesman.

'Up there, McKenna!' Blaise Trezise held his beer can up to the heavens as the Collingwood full forward rode the back of his opponent to take a speckie.

The MCG roared. McKenna lined up a drop punt then booted the ball straight through the sticks.

Melanie screamed and jumped into her grandfather's arms as a sea of black and white colours flooded the arena. The old man sat down on the bench and wiped his forehead with a hanky.

'Your great grandfather noticed that the diggers started playing a similar game to the blacks on the gold fields. When the poor buggers were booted off their land, it reminded William of the stories his grandfather had told him about the English doing the same to the Cornish. You bloody white maggot umpire! Our people were robbed of their land, their language and their dignity, Mel, just like the poor old blackfellas were.' Blaise's ancient eyes moistened.

'You know that the MCG is built on a corroboree ground? Carn the Pies!' The old man belched then took another swig from his can. 'I reckon there's a divine justice in that the game we love comes from a blackfellas' ritual.'

Blaise couldn't tell his granddaughter about the aching emptiness inside his soul. Even though his wife Gwen had died a decade ago, Blaise always felt her presence with each hobbling step he took around his musty house. A small cloud of dust rose every time the old man sat in his armchair. He'd complain to his wife's ghost about how everyone these days ran around like blue-arsed flies just to make a quid. His father had taught him to be satisfied with the simple things of life. Blaise passed this wisdom onto his family. The old man asked Gwen if people really needed all the latest mod cons? Did it make them any happier? Gwen slowly shook her head as she sat on the couch below the window. A silver sun dissolved behind her.

Blaise despaired over the way his country had become an outpost of America. Even his beloved sport had been taken over by the money-grubbers. Christ, something's got to be wrong with the world when the Magpies suffered from a long drought of grand finals victories.

Blaise slowly got up from his chair to lay his head upon his wife's lap. He sighed deeply as she stroked his hair. That's how Arthur found him the next day, with a hint of a smile and sleeping as peaceful as a baby.

Melanie's labour dragged all through the night and following morning. A foot dangled from the birth canal when the obstetrician broke her water. Melanie lay sprawled in the post-op room, with her long limbs; she looked like a horse that had been hit by a truck. The caesarean was her first operation.

When Arthur and Lilla whispered to their daughter, she could only whimper. They visited their grandchild in a humicrib that afternoon.

Arthur's heart broke while they pricked the baby's foot for a blood test. The little one's face turned beetroot as he screamed from his first experience of pain. Lilla stuck her hand into the humicrib and encouraged the baby to wrap his tiny claw around her finger.

Melanie saw her son after regaining consciousness that night. The little boy had inherited the Tresize blue eyes, red hair and huge head circumference. Melanie cooed as they placed her baby upon her chest. She decided to call him Blaise. A teary-eyed Arthur said that his father was smiling down on them.

Although exhausted, Melanie loved the three o'clock feeds in the morning where the only sounds were Blaise's gulps and sighs and the magpies singing in the gum tree outside. There was a calm to this nightly ritual unlike anything she'd experienced before. Apart from the birds, it was if the outside world no longer existed. Her grandfather smiled in the lamplight on her beside cabinet.

When he turned six months, Blaise stopped crying for his morning feed. Melanie lay in bed and chuckled when she'd heard her son trilling away in his bedroom. She entered his doorway to the sight of him kicking his tiny legs and shaking his arms as he pointed his pink face to the ceiling and sang out a tune similar to a magpie.

The birds joined them each morning in the courtyard for morning tea. Melanie would balance a tray with a pot of tea and biscuits together with a couple of slices of bread for the birds. Her neighbour's giant oak tree had turned. Autumn was Melanie's favourite time of year. She loved the way the cooling sun stretched shadows across her garden. The days were always blue and warm, the nights crisp, perfect sleeping weather, which was what Blaise did a lot of. Her courtyard garden shimmered with gold light.

The magpies always appeared on the front fence then swooped down at the crumbs Melanie tossed onto the brick path. After having his fill, the parent magpie would jump on to Melanie and Blaise's wooden garden bench. He'd point his beak up to the dreaming sun, puff out his chest and sing. When Blaise turned from his mother's breast to smile at the bird, Melanie saw her grandfather's blue gleaming eyes.

Four autumns passed. Australia fought two Asians wars on the same side as America and Melanie and Blaise continued their morning tea in the courtyard with the magpies. The boy would crouch down to hand feed them.

One morning as Melanie lay dozing in bed, she heard someone tapping on the front door. When she opened it, a magpie greeted her demanding to be fed. Each summer saw the parent magpies introduce new babies to the Tresizes. This year there was a big fat grey-feathered bird Blaise christened Squeak, and another smaller bird with gentle brown eyes who went by the name of Beep. Melanie drew pictures of the magpie family and stuck them up on her son's bedroom wall.

Blaise spent a lot of his waking hours outside with the birds. As Melanie did her housework, she'd sometimes spot her son perched on a branch of a tree with his four mates. Blaise was now a perfect mimic. When the neighbours heard him sing, they found it hard to tell his voice from the magpies. Blaise sang with joy, tossing back his blond head, sticking out his chest and stretching his shining eyes to sing a full-throated tune up to the gods of the blue sky. Melanie beamed from her kitchen window.

Sometimes it was suspiciously quiet outside. Melanie would go out into the garden to find the magpies, perched on one foot with their tiny white eyelids down. Blaise would be balancing on one leg on a branch nearby with his eyes closed and a big grin on his face. When Melanie finished her chores, she'd play Magpies with Blaise, where they'd make a nest on his bed with spare blankets and pillows. She'd put a piece of Lego in her mouth then pretend to feed her squawking flapping son by placing it into his lips with her teeth.

Blaise loved walking around the house in his bare feet, bobbing his head and tucking his hands under his armpits to make it appear as if he had wings. The little boy caught a bad cold once and refused to put his slippers and socks on. When Melanie asked him why, he said he didn't want to lose his magpie claws. Melanie didn't push it.

When Blaise was invited to his first superhero birthday party, Melanie drew number thirty-five onto a piece of cloth then stitched it onto the back of his Collingwood guernsey. All the other children went as Batman, Superman or Spiderman. Blaise went as the legendary Collingwood forward Peter Daicos. As Melanie introduced her son to parents at the party, Blaise insisted that his name was Squeak the magpie.

Arthur loved to play kick to kick with his Blaise out in the backyard while the four magpies watched in the gum tree. The old man praised his grandson's every kick. The little boy's face lit up after Melanie, Lilla and Arthur clapped and cheered him for taking his first mark. Slowly but surely, Blaise learnt how to throw his young body into the sky and catch the sun like his ancestors did all those years ago on the gold fields of Ballarat.

Melanie put on a brave face but cried in the house by herself after taking her son to school. Blaise had said that now he was a big boy in uniform he no longer needed to hold her hand when they crossed the road.

She took her son to his first footy match at the MCG and showed him the scar trees at Yarra Park. Blaise listened as his mother told him how the Wurundjeri made canoes out of the ancient red gums. The little boy imagined what the place looked like before crowds and cars.

His mother's loneliness eased when the teacher said Blaise was the only child who noticed the birds in the playground and that his classmates loved listening to his bird stories. Melanie continued breaking bread for her magpies. Squeak and Beep eventually left the nest, but at least the adults still had each other for company.

The Doghouse

I'm in the doghouse again.

'Thanks for nothing!' my old man shouts at me down the other end of the line.

'You're very welcome,' I reply before he slams the phone down.

He'd asked if I could store eight removal boxes of my sister's stuff in my garage. My oldest sister was breaking up with the same guy for the umpteenth time and needed somewhere to put her crap. The family had done the same to me ten years ago when the old man and my uncle Clarrie suddenly rocked up in my driveway with a trailer load of my sister's rubbish.

Dad was moving to Mooroolbark and after some major excavations, had found two ancient tables that my sister hadn't used for donkeys. I couldn't say no to the sight of them walking up the driveway with my Auntie Alice's ancient disassembled oak table, so they put it with another laminated pink formica table in my garage. Dad reckoned they'd only be there for a short time. I threw them out in last year's hard rubbish drive.

The old man came out with the same old garbage again this time. 'Your sister's stuff will only be there for a short time.'

'Dad, she said the same thing last time. The tables ended up our garage for ages.'

'What are you doing this arvo?'

'Watching Collingwood with Tim. Why?'

'I could do with a hand up here. I'm trying to make room in the garage for your sister's things.'

'It's a bit short notice, isn't it?' My eleven-year-old son and I had bought party pies, sausage rolls and pizza shapes to watch the traditional Queen's birthday holiday clash between Collingwood and Melbourne.

Besides, my old man never throws anything out. When he had a hard rubbish drive a couple of months ago, he asked me to help him.

'Are you actually going to throw anything out this time?'

'Well…'

I helped my dad move house from Nunawading to Mooroolbark. Getting stuff out of the house wasn't too much of a drama, but he didn't touch the garage until settlement day. Our family always had a two-car garage; trouble was, you could never fit a car in because they were always chockers with Dad's crap. So we started on settlement day. The old man had row upon row of steel shelves loaded with things in boxes, tins and jars.

'Can we chuck this in the skip, Dad?' It was a large jar full of the small rectangular plastic thingies you click on to your shaver so you don't cut yourself.

'Nah! You never know when they'll come in handy.' The old man took the jar and stored it in Uncle Clarrie's van.

I came across a big jar full of plastic pens without the middle bits in them. 'Chuck 'em out, Dad?'

'No, son. You'll find they can be pretty useful as well.'

Uncle Clarrie raised his blue eyes to the grey sky as into his van the empty pen cases went. And so on and on all frigging afternoon it went, until the van bulged with Dad's crap. I got an idea of how Howard Carter must have felt excavating Tutankhamen's tomb. Once I got through the first row of stuff on the shelves, there would be another row of crap behind it, then another row of crap behind that as well.

Because Mum had given me fairly clear instructions that morning: 'Throw as much of your old man's shit out as you can.'

I attempted to go beyond his all-seeing eye and attack the spare bedroom full of junk. Every family house I'd lived in had a spare bedroom full of the old man's junk. I opened up the door to be greeted by a Himalayan mountain range of crap. There were cardboard and foam boxes stacked right up to the ceiling, old stereo and radio parts, microphone stands, enough old lamps and ceiling lights to open up a light display at Bunnings, radio magazines dating back to the 1950s, spare shelves and brackets, dusty rolls of carpet, car doors, old cupboards with avalanches of junk pouring out of them when you opened the door et cetera, et-bloody-cetera.

With Mum's words ringing in my ears, I snuck up and turfed some bloody lights into the gaping mouth of the skip.

'Who threw that in!' shouted the old man, circling the skip like a bloody hawk.

When I shrugged, Dad turned his glaring brown eyes to our Pommy neighbour, who'd foolishly volunteered to help us with the move.

'It wasn't me, Barry, honest!' The poor bugger froze like a rabbit trapped in the headlights.

I suffered from my second nervous breakdown as it took us three weeks after settlement to finally clear the old man's garage. My first nervous breakdown occurred years ago when we moved from Bulleen to Nunawading. Uncle Clarrie wasn't available that time (funny that), so it was just me and Dad and a trailer. I somehow managed to help Dad clear the garage and the spare bedroom full of junk only to discover he'd had stored a layer of megacrap under the house! I was almost tearful as I crept in the dirt to pull out the walls to our old above-ground swimming pool (they'd make good insulation), swallowing hard when we pulled out the old solid metal mast of a broken clothes line (handy if a pipe breaks) and an emotional wreck by the time we hauled out half a dozen old Morris engines (they're collector's items, you know).

Still, it wasn't all doom and gloom. I remember laughing when our cocky chatted from his cage on the trailer to people when they pulled up behind us at an intersection. Cocky was Dad's best mate; he used to sit on his shoulder and chat to Dad all night out in the garage. The old man also had this mad, fuzzy headed friend who only surfaced when we moved. His loony eyes always lit up every time he saw Dad's crap. 'I feel like all my Christmases have come at once,' he'd say as he'd shovel Dad's shit into the back of his panel van. (To this day, I never figured out who this bloke was and why he was given unfettered access to

Dad's stuff.) He once ripped off a foam lid of one of Dad's boxes, put it in his mouth, then chirped, 'I'm so happy I'm foaming at the mouth.'

But the funniest thing I ever saw was when Uncle Clarrie finally completed his shuttle of shit from Nunawading to Mooroolbark. The Mooroolbark garage was full to capacity, so the weatherproof foam boxes splashed out into the backyard. Dad had promised Mum that they would be able to get their cars into the new garage. When Mum realised this wasn't going to happen and when she saw Uncle Clarrie and Dad storing boxes out in the backyard, she stormed out of the front door up to the van. And with her head stooped down in rage, her arms flapping, in the words of my wife, Julie, she looked like an enraged goose as she hissed out, 'You're such a selfish, selfish old bastard!' Such was my family's introduction to the neighbours of Mooroolbark.

I never had an old man; he was always out there in the frigging garage. He was a speaker rigged up in the lounge room, where we'd flick a switch and say, 'Tea's ready, Dad.'

'Righto,' he'd reply, come in, have his meal, then go straight back out again. He'd only appear in the house at eleven at night for a read. When once I asked him why, he replied, 'It's the only time the house is quiet.'

Admittedly, both of my sisters are drama queens so, in some ways, I don't blame him. He used to call them the 'climatics', because we always got 'four seasons in one day' with the both of them.

I remember being shocked once when I visited a friend, Peter, and his old man was sitting on the couch talking to his family when it wasn't meal time! I was even more stunned when he came out in the backyard to play cricket with us. Christ, old Barry boy never did any of that with me. Most baby boomers that I talk with admit their old man was the exactly the same. I can understand if they were out there earning an extra quid, but most of them pottered away neglecting their family by doing bugger all. My poor old mum's a social butterfly who's always having her wings clipped by old Barry because all he wants to do is hover over his work bench and tinker away with his bits and bobs.

To be fair to Barry, I can remember a few times when his stuff did come in handy. When I did a front headlight to my 1972 Torana, the old man got up on his ladder, pulled out a box, and there it was, the exact same headlight in perfectly good nick. When Julie's car stereo speaker went in her 1991 Corolla, Dad had a replacement one stacked away in one of his foam boxes. Julie and I laugh when we look back on it now, because over the years practically everything fell off her Corolla except for Dad's firmly screwed-in speaker. It was a solid as Uluru.

When we buried Barry's father Tim, my pop, I can remember standing next to my old man with tears streaming down my face. Dad turned to me and said, 'I wish I could do that but I don't know how to.' I hugged the poor bugger.

I cry at the drop of a hat; I get it from my mum. Dad used to call me a sook when I was a little tacker. Dad's a child of the Great Depression. They never had the toys that kids have got today. Poor old Pop worked on the susso, pushing wheelbarrows of clay around a quarry from dawn to dusk. So they had nothing. Maybe that explains Dad's behaviour. Whenever anything comes his way, he grabs and never lets go.

From what I heard, Tim was a hard old taskmaster. Nana used to brag about how she never laid a finger on Barry. But Mum told me that when Dad did do something wrong, Nana used to lock him up in his room until Pop came home to thrash the pants off him. I sometimes picture a terrified young Barry waiting in his room, and then the horror of a boy being strapped around his legs until they're red by his father's belt.

Maybe the garage is Barry's refuge from emotional rawness and the only way he can express his love is by doing a job for you. I remember being on the verge of a genuine nervous breakdown when after four years of study at uni, I threw the towel in and decided I wasn't going to into teaching, plus the woman I adored didn't love me, then my frigging 1968 Cortina's engine blew up. Barry rebuilt the car for me from parts he had out in the garage; the old Cortina rocketed on forever.

To be fair to Pop, he taught me the important basics that Barry never showed me, like how to hammer a nail and bowl a flipper. Pop and Nana took me to see Collingwood. They used to come down and watch me when I played for the local team. Pop and I became really close after he gave me the letters, postcards and medals from his brother Edward, who died on the Western Front during the so-called Great War. Pop's eyes became moist when he explained to me that Edward was his favourite brother. Poor old Pop didn't know how to cry either.

I like to think I'm not as bad as Dad when it comes to garages. I have an extensive collection of Tasmanian beer bottles and cans on the wall next to the workbench in my single-car garage. Pop's ancient work vice sits on my bench; I nicked it from his decaying garage down in Rosebud when I discovered they were going to pull our old family holiday house down. Dad reckons the vice was built by Pop's father, the original Tim. I sometimes wonder if he stood next to it tearless in his garage when he heard of the death of his son Edward.

I have only one cupboard half full of crap. When Julie sometimes says that I'm just as bad a hoarder as my old man, I remind her that at least we can get our car in. Like my friend Peter's father, I'm never out in the garage. I've planted lots of bushes and creepers around mine so that over the years it'll hopefully blend into the garden.

Tim and I knock off some party pies and sausage rolls, then jump off the couch and abuse the screen. Like all the bloody games between Collingwood and Melbourne, no matter where they are on the ladder, it's always close. I don't call my son a sook as he cries when Melbourne threaten to beat us because I'm doing the same thing. It's half time, so we go out into the street and play kick to kick. Midwinter Melbourne puts on her typical show of a freezing north wind battling grey clouds pregnant with rain and snow.

Dad's probably in his icebox of a garage shuffling his boxes and listening to the game on the radio. I wonder if he's still in a stink with me? Who knows? But I bet he's probably content out there tinkering away time.

Tim's pink face is beaming after I praise him for taking a spectacular mark. Life can be good in the doghouse.

The Spinebill

The spinebills have returned; they always do this time of year. Another summer's about to die, thank God! The bird's trilling is the first thing you notice; it sounds like a mini machine gun. (If there's such a thing as a mini machine gun.)

I noticed the spinebill during the first autumn I was home looking after my son, Tim. When I took three years off on family leave, I discovered important things I'd overlooked when I worked full time. For instance, signs of when the seasons are changing; this tiny bird's arrival is the one of the first indications that autumn is on her way and we're near the equinox, a time our ancestors celebrated with great gusto. We probably still do. During Saint Patrick's Day and Easter, some drink, others pray, some reflect, others do sweet nothing; the seasons change, according to the tilt of our blue planet and the angle of the sun's ray.

Thanks to global warming, Melbourne's had weeks of unusual tropical weather. When I was a kid in summer, we had a bearable desert heat that was always swept away by a cool change by at least the fourth day. This weather pattern has passed now; I think it vanished during the last drought.

My long-dead bird-watching neighbour once told me the spinebills make their way across the treacherous waters of Bass Strait to return to the native bushes in our outer eastern suburbs. A sprinkling of plants in our neighbourhood gardens and parks are all that's left of a purple-tinged forest that once stretched all the way from the bay to the mountains.

The spinebill's whistle always makes me smile. Come now autumn, with your dreaming golden light, stretching shadows and crisp, deep-sleeping nights. Three spinebills dart like fairy wrens around my old grevillea bush in the driveway; their markings remind me of native finches. Begone stinking hot summer, they chirrup through their curved black beaks. How long do these little souls live for? Perhaps they're the children or the grandchildren of the birds I first noticed in the same bush a decade ago. Their knowledge of this old plant lives through the generations.

It's been a summer I want to forget. The first week of January was heavenly. I spent it with my wife, Alana, and twelve-year-old son down at Port Fairy. Like migratory birds, we always return to this neck of the woods every new year. We spent most afternoons swimming in the Southern Ocean. (It's curious how we always use the word 'spend' when we talk about the passing of time. It sounds like a transaction, which I suppose it is; a transaction with mortality.)

My darling boy, Tim, had his first swimming lessons before we left town. We delayed him having to put his head under water, because he was born with a cleft palette and smaller than normal Eustachian tubes. He's undergone twelve operations. But his twelfth was called off two weeks before Christmas because the surgeon ran out of time. We got to the hospital at seven in the morning; our boy was prepped and put in his blue gown at ten; the surgeon would ring roughly every forty minutes to say he was ready for the next child. We agonisingly watched a succession of children climb into the hospital trolley to be wheeled off and hoped our son would be next. But at two-thirty, the surgeon rang to tell the nurse they'd run out of time. The ringing of the ward phone is torture; it reminds me of when the Spitfire pilots waited for the phone call to tell them whether they were going to scramble or if tea was up.

The surgeon told the nurse to let us know he was coming up to explain why he couldn't operate. We three waited for another eternal three-quarters of an hour. During this time, a fat bogan couple came in to put the stupid telly on, which nobody watched, then proceeded to tell their little boy he was a scaredy cat because he didn't want an operation. Why are people like that allowed to procreate? Why do hospitals allow manic, moronic, commercial television to dominate the waiting room? I'd had a largely successful day where I'd managed to keep the idiot box off or kept the stupid volume down, but when the two fatties came, it was the last straw. I told the nurse it was pointless waiting only for the surgeon to come up and tell us why he couldn't operate. We chuckled as we left because Tim told us he'd felt like he'd been just let out of jail.

He swished like a dolphin down at Port Fairy. He loved torpedoing though the foaming ocean water. I showed him how to dive below a threatening wave and how to boogie board. We'd chat and laugh as we waited for the best wave to catch. His young face lit up with pure joy when he felt the sensation of being picked up and carried all the way back to shore. Trouble was, the hospital rang up a week after the debacle and booked us in for the second week of January, a week before Tim's birthday. We didn't have the heart to tell him straight away and thought it best to let him know only a few days before the operation. So, bathe on in merman bliss, my sea-caressed boy, my sunny shining blue-eyed son.

On the last day at Port Fairy, we discovered our old cat, Moogal, had died. Our neighbours frantically tried to ring us on the second day of our trip to consult us about whether Moogal should be put down or not. The second of January was the hottest day of summer, over forty-two degrees. Poor old Moogal had a cancerous tumour in her stomach which ruptured in the extreme heat. Our neighbours found her out in the backyard struggling to get up and walk. Moogal could barely breathe when they rushed her to the emergency clinic. For some unknown reason, we didn't get their phone messages.

Alana checked our mobile every night. Maybe it was because we were out of range – Port Fairy's hundreds of miles from town – or perhaps the God we don't believe in had intervened so that our seaside holiday wasn't ruined. Who knows? I told my wife it was karma, something I increasingly believe in as I get older. The idea that there's another life force out there that ploughs on irrespective of how we think or feel and it's only with the benefit of time that we understand why things turn out the way they do.

We nearly didn't buy Moogal (her name was Aboriginal for pretty girl).Alana was interested in her older sister, a pretty white tortoiseshell who was one of a family of five in the pet shop. Moogal, a black tortoiseshell; was the runt of the litter who kept boxing up her brothers and sisters in self-defence. I admired her pluck, so we bought her. We already had two tortoiseshells that turned out to be extremely jealous of the interloper. Moogal managed to hold her own against their repeatedly nasty attacks.

We'd been married two years. Moogal was our first kitten. Alana now readily admits Moogal was her baby substitute. When we moved house, we lost her for six weeks. Our puss had somehow managed to attach herself to the chassis of my car. When I went to buy some petrol, I heard something bumping behind me, then through the rear-view mirror I saw my cat race across Canterbury Road. I slammed the brakes on and ran to where I last saw her near the railway track. I searched the scrub forever. Alana and I looked for her every night for six weeks. We photocopied hundreds of pamphlets (at work) and letter-boxed the area around the train line. My mate Luke told me cats seldom stray from where you last saw them. Alana and I knocked on people's doors, searched through gardens, crawled beneath houses, and responded to people's phone calls. While everybody else was secure in their homes watching the telly, we were out in the darkness, catching colds, losing weight and sometimes crying at night.

Alana got a phone call from a lady who worked for the local swimming pool company and told us she'd seen a cat fitting Moogal's description sometimes sunning herself on one of the pools decks. Alana and I were a bit numb by now because we'd had calls about black cats like this before which had all turned out to be fruitless. (We even had some stupid kids ringing us up pretending they had Moogal and made meowing noises.) Alana brought a piece of chicken with her and started calling Moogal's name. A furry black sniffing head cautiously appeared from below the decking of a pool. It was our girl!

Alana cuddled her then raced off to the vet. Somehow, Moogal had managed to get her collar stuck underneath the base of her front leg, the rubbing created an infected wound full of maggots. The infection was life-threatening, so we had to leave her at the vets for a week. We nicknamed her Lazarus after that. Luke was right: the swimming pool company was only a couple of yards away from where I last saw her.

She was never a lap cat but a rather grumpy puss who barely tolerated a pat before biting you. She must have known towards the end, because she'd always jump up on the couch and head-butt my hand to demand a pat. My last novel was written with Moogal sleeping and purring next to me. However, she also became incontinent; our lounge regularly stank of cat piss, shit and vomit which I inevitably had to clean up before getting stuck into my story. I miss her smell when I write these days. The couch pillow next to me is empty.

We threw our bags in the house after the long drive back from Port Fairy then collected our cat's frozen body from the vet. When we unwrapped her, we discovered she was in the foetal position. The same position our ancestors buried their loved ones thousands of years ago, with food, drink and prized possessions by their side to accompany them to the afterlife. Moogal was in this position in the last photo Alana took of her before we left for Port Fairy. Moogal used to love curling herself up into a ball and sleep in the afternoon sun in our backyard. Our first kitten died in the arms of our gentle neighbour, Amanda, who confirmed she was in the foetal position and had a peaceful death.

Our other two cats were curious about Moogal when we buried her. Zoe, our oldest tortoiseshell, crawled down the hole I'd dug to sniff Moogal's body. When she got out of the hole, she bit our other black tortoiseshell, Evie, on the backside as if to say, 'Go pay your last respects, woman!' Evie wearily went over to Moogal's grave and sniffed. The vet was right when she said both girls would be subdued for the next few days. Cats know; that's why I love them. I couldn't hold back the tears when Tim read the words to George Harrison's 'All Things Must Pass' over our cat's grave. I pictured Moogal as she used to scuttle across the kitchen in our rental flat. She was an expert fly catcher; if we ever had an annoying blowy in our house, Moogal always caught it. Alana lit incense sticks and placed them around Moogal's grave. Tim found a rock that looked exactly like a headstone, wrote an M on it and gently placed it at the top of the grave.

Our boy had to wait three-and-a-half hours before his last operation. He wailed like a banshee on the morning of his operation. We got to the hospital at seven, encountered a bit of bureaucratic bullshit by being sent to the wrong ward, then waited. Tim was very good. We attempted to keep him busy with his Nintendo but then he'd break down and cry, Alana and I tried to comfort him as best we could, by emphasising this was his last operation and that he'd got Puffing Billy to look forward to on his birthday in a week's time. The man finally arrived with the trolley. Alana and I were right there by his side as they wheeled him to the operating theatre on the floor above us. Alana gowned up and went in with him as they gave him the anaesthetic. My heart was in my mouth.

Tim had this red rash all over his body as he lay in recovery. By the time the anaesthetist arrived to investigate, it had disappeared. As our son regained consciousness, we whispered how brave he was and that this was his last operation.

Sometimes now when we go out with friends, he holds water in his mouth then bows his head right down to prove the water no longer leaks through the roof of his mouth into his nose. Alana and I speculate that perhaps it was fated we became his parents. You see, both of us have been and still are outsiders. Alana migrated from America when she was a girl. She's tall and skinny and as a result was mercilessly stirred by her Australian classmates. I've always been a poet, a teller of stories and was regularly poofter-bashed at school. So we understand our boy when he says he feels different. We try to teach our son not to dwell too much upon his cleft palette and that you must keep moving, just like the tiny birds who overcome the wildness of Bass Strait to then sing about the glory of life in our driveway during the birth of autumn.

A Touch of Madness

The horn blowing and brake slamming seemed to go forever, but lasted maybe thirty seconds. People raised their heads and pulled off their ear pieces to stare out the window. Our train screeched to a sudden halt in the winter darkness out in the middle of nowhere. Judging by the chatter and gasps, the passengers knew what had just happened. The driver climbed down the cabin steps and searched the tracks below our carriage with his torch. Some people whimpered in the silence.

'He's looking on the wrong side.' A neatly bearded, suited, passenger standing next to the door opposite me held his hands over his eyes as he stared into blackness below him. 'You probably don't want to look down there.' He faced us then nodded over his shoulder. His calm face struggled to control the horror. His eyes were full of fear yet there was relief in them as well. Perhaps he was thanking God it wasn't him.

A work colleague of mine heard the body go under the train two years ago and had to take some time off. It altered him; he was a bit of a cold fish but now he seems more vulnerable. Yet this time, there was no impact sound as the train shuddered to a halt. But there was obviously a body lying below our carriage in the freezing cold outside. The driver jumped back into the cabin to announce over the microphone that there had been an accident. The silence was broken by cries and people ringing their mobile phones.

I'll go back to my book, I told myself, but found it impossible to focus on the words. Others put their heads down and pretended to do the same. The mobile phone callers shouted as they repeated there'd been an accident and whined how they'd probably be stuck on the train for hours. People speculated about where we were. The consensus was we were stranded somewhere between Mitcham and Heatherdale, the outer eastern suburbs of the city. We sat for what seemed an eternity until there suddenly appeared luminous vests, helmets and torches searching everywhere on the tracks below. You couldn't see their faces but judging by their bodies, the emergency workers all appeared to be big middle-aged men.

The bearded passenger pressed the emergency button but after no response he knocked on the door window and pointed directly below where he was standing. He quietly told the rest of us that he'd seen a body without legs, but also that it was jet black outside and hoped that perhaps the lower part of the body was hidden behind a bush. He slowly shook his head as he uttered, 'What a place to do it. The last thing you'd see was a blackberry bush before you died.'

What a place indeed, hidden far away from your fellow human beings. Beyond all hope, with just one last grisly task left in your fevered brain, grasping for the release of death. You couldn't get anywhere bleaker than an empty, prickly paddock in the outer suburbs in between stations. Away from the breath and bustle of your fellow human beings, miles from the nearest road. He'd jolted a trainload of passengers out of their everyday existence. How did he do it? Did he lie on the track or walk into the comet light of the speeding train?

Some women panicked, some men became anxious as the emergency workers made a half-circle around us. A young fair-haired man sitting directly across me kept shuffling in his chair while he scrolled down his mobile phone. He mumbled he was in the train company's website and it mentioned the accident but didn't go into any detail.

An ambulance suddenly appeared at the top of the paddock, slowly reversing until it was level with our carriage. The young fair-haired man looked at the cover of my book, which was a history of how they put man on the moon.

'You know that's supposed to have not happened?' By the scared look on his face, I could tell he was desperate for conversation.

'My father-in-law used to work for NASA. He helped to design the guidance system on the lunar module that got man there. NASA employed thousands of people. How could they all be liars? He reckons everyone in charge was mad.'

'Oh really!' He gave me a surprised smile.

'He said one manager used to walk around with a can of sardines in his top pocket which he'd crack open every time there was a crisis. Another manager never sat down but used to lie horizontally across the top of his desk.'

'I suppose you would have to have a touch of madness to do that job,' replied the young fair-haired fella, with a twinkle in his eye. By now, all the torch-bearing emergency workers had reached the spot pointed to by our bearded passenger.

A tall policeman marched in and instructed us to evacuate our carriage. I unfortunately lost contact with the passenger I'd started up a conversation with and slowly found a seat in the carriage behind the driver's cabin. I could still make out the ambulance. The emergency workers carried a stretcher to the accident site. Should I keep looking or turn away? The answer to this question came as the stretcher was lifted back towards the ambulance. On it I saw the back of a bald, shaved head of a man who looked like he might only be in his thirties. Then I saw him waving his arm.

'It's still alive!' someone shouted.

I imagined the impact, then the horror of the realisation that he'd survived; the pain, the damage done to his body by the iron wheels of the train. Another emergency worker came down to the railway track with a large yellow plastic bag; it seems our bearded passenger had seen things correctly.

At last, we were told by the policeman we could evacuate the train and that buses had been arranged for every ten minutes at Mitcham Station. We stood and queued and slowly made our way to the driver's cabin. For a man who had just been involved in a major accident, he seemed almost chirpy as he instructed us to turn our backs and grip the bars and step down one by one down off the train. The dark cabin was almost tranquil. I thought of Neil Armstrong and how he steered the lunar module over a boulder-strewn landscape with only seconds of fuel left. The police took our bags off of us then gripped our ankles to guide us down the train driver's ladder. We were greeted by darkness and drizzle. There were plenty of police to guide us when we stepped off the tracks to the nearest road. An old woman behind me grumbled on about how there should be floodlights so we could see where we're going. I ignored her just as I'd ignored several other people who had complained that night. A soul had probably perished and they couldn't see beyond their own noses. I turned my head to the sight of hundreds of people queuing to get off the metallic train; it reminded me of a queen insect disgorging its young.

Naturally there was no shuttle of buses by the time we arrived at Mitcham Station. There was a public phone. I tossed up whether to ring home or not. Knowing that my wife would be at yoga or, even if she'd stayed home, she wouldn't be able to pick me up because the traffic was horrendous, and I couldn't give my thirteen-year-old son a time when I'd come home, I decided to wait for a bus. A fellow middle-aged old codger came up to me and asked whether he'd get into trouble because he hadn't validated his ticket yet. Our laughter drew another middle-aged old codger and we decided that we three would gang up against any burly ticket inspectors who came our way.

We finally caught a sardine-packed bus to Ringwood. One of my fellow middled-aged mates stood next to the front window to crack jokes and help guide the bus driver, who was unfamiliar with this part of town. When we arrived at Ringwood, railway workers escorted us to the correct platform to catch the train home. An extremely overweight young woman loudly crapped onto one off the staff members how she had to wait forty minutes for a bus, I almost went over to her to tell her to shut up.

I looked at the sign as I boarded the Belgrave train to realise I had to wait another half hour before it took off. I tried to read my book again but was drawn across the carriage to listening to this happy silver-bearded old fella chatting to a friend. He seemed blissfully unaware of the attempted suicide. He talked of his love for fishing and how he never drank while casting a line, but enjoyed a beer when he wasn't. (I was determined to have a beer or three when I got home.) He made wooden toys out in his garage for charity groups and never charged for them. He showed his friend a photo he kept in his wallet of a hospitalised disabled four-year-old girl, and mentioned she had a look of half smiling, half in fear as she held one of his toys.

Half smiling, half in fear, the look of the bearded passenger, the train driver, the young man who spoke with me, the police who escorted me off the train, the disabled little girl: it was a lesson I was to relearn – probably the best way to deal with adversity is with a smile.

There was no one home when I came through the door with my half dozen beers. There was a written note on the kitchen bench that my wife and son were across the road with our neighbours. My wife had gone to yoga, my son across the road, when it was obvious I wasn't coming home soon. (So much for the need for a mobile phone in an emergency.) Life rolls on, or screams to a halt, regardless of our needs.

There was nothing in the news the next day. Someone had tried to kill himself, a whole train network was disrupted, there was traffic chaos everywhere, but it wasn't reported. A discreet article came out in the paper a month after the accident. It talked about black spots, clusters on the railway that are known for where young people lie on the tracks waiting to die.

I sometimes recall that night when I hear the sound of a train horn in the distance or study the steel wheels of a train on my way to work. I often think of that poor man on the tracks and the gesture of his arm. Was he waving or was it a reflex? Did he die after being cut in half or did he somehow get through it? Was he being wheeled around a hospital? God, you have my pity. Lecturing is a waste of time. I should know; I've been through the same dark region. I have the scars to prove it. My wife knew I'd returned when she saw the gleam come back to my eyes.

Neil Armstrong died while I wrote this story. The intelligent recluse, I'll never forget the look on his face after his moonwalk, the smiling man on the moon. Children know all about the wonder of life, some of us lose that awe, yet we're sometimes given the opportunity to relearn. A touch of madness can be a good thing.

Almost the Final Frontier

At last I've got an afternoon all to myself! My thirteen-year-old son, Tim, is having a mate over to play with and I've got most of my domestic garbage out of the way. The clothes are hanging out to dry in the backyard. The bellbirds are chirping. I've opened up the house to get some fresh spring air in; I might try and write a story or polish some poems.

You beauty! I think I'll try a new story. What'll I write about? I don't know until my son comes into the lounge room and asks me to look at the plug attachment to his Fender. It's come loose. I should be able to fix it, no worries. It's a fiddly bloody thin,g though! Tim's mate Daniel arrives and they're talking in the kitchen to our pet cockatiel, Jim, named after Captain James T. Kirk, of the Star Ship *Enterprise*. He's a sweet-natured thing, who really adores human company. He loves me to rub the back of his neck with my beard. One day I'll probably get cockatiel flu and my beard will drop off. Two orange butterflies circle dance in the driveway. The boys rush to play outside with Tim's Nerf guns. Jim's chirping happily away in the kitchen but suddenly he's screeching from what sounds like outside!

Tim charges into the lounge room to shout that Jim's escaped out through the back door! Fek! There goes the bloody afternoon. I place his guitar on the couch and race out to the backyard. Although it's distant, we can still hear his whistle. I tell Tim and Daniel to grab Jim's cage and we'll try and find him. We end up at our neighbour's house two doors down. No one's home, so Tim goes around and Daniel climbs over our neighbour's large wire side fence. I'm too wide to go around it and reluctant to climb over it because there's all this loose sharp pants-ripping wire on the top. So I stand there and direct the boys. I shout to Tim to keep calling to the bird, let him know we're still around and tell Daniel to keep banging the door on Jim's cage. Maybe these familiar sounds will attract him back.

I'm just about to go home to change into my tracky pants when my neighbour rocks up.

'Are you waiting for someone?' my neighbour cautiously asks as he steps out of his car.

I realise I must look like a prize prawn malingering near his side gate. I explain to him what's happened and he ushers me out into his backyard. He has this beautiful old oak tree that's over fifty feet high. Bloody Jim's in there somewhere. We all scan the tree until Tim points and we can just make out his little silhouette right up on the top of the tree. The little gobshite's got his crest up and he's preening himself! Is he nervous or celebrating his new-found freedom? He responds to every one of Tim's whistles with a little chirp of acknowledgement and looks down at us sometimes when Daniel bangs the cage door. Tim's on the verge of tears, I tell him not to cry but keep calling to the pea brain so he'll know we're still around for him. I attempt to whistle the ditty 'Pop goes the weasel'. Jim responds to all our sounds. Tim wants to climb up the tree but I tell him it's too dangerous and besides he might scare him off. A band of tension stretches tightly across my forehead. Little fekking gobshite! Stop pruning yourself, feather brain, and get down the fekking tree! I could be writing a story by now, bugger it!

My neighbour asks me if I'd like a cuppa.

'Yes please,' I reply.

He tries to engage me in small talk when he brings the mug out but senses I'm too stressed out and goes back inside to watch the car racing, I go back to 'Pop goes the weasel'.

We've been in this Mexican stand-off for about an hour when a couple of bellbirds suddenly appear to harass Jim. He screams as he takes off with two bellbirds in close proximity to his little fluffy arse. He soars across the street towards the Housing Commission estate. It looks like something out of the Battle of Britain, a couple of Spitfires swooping upon a sitting-duck German bomber.

I pick up Jim's cage, say a quick goodbye to my neighbour and follow the boys across the road. Again the little gobshite's perched on top of the highest branch of an ancient gum tree. The bellbirds shuffle in a branch below him and chirp aggressively. Jim cries as he takes off then zooms over the roof of our house with two of the fighters on his tail. What can we do but follow him? I have a huge knot in my stomach by now, Tim's on the verge of tears again and Daniel looks really worried. The poor bugger came over for a play and this rubbish happens. The sky's getting grey; a good thing, I think to myself: the rain will restrict his flight.

I remember about thirty years ago when my white pet budgie, Gough, got out. He flew into my neighbour's gum tree and sat there for an eternity. My neighbour suggested that I climb my dad's garage with the garden house and spray him out of the tree. It bloody well worked! Gough plummeted like a white rock when I hit him with the water, my neighbour scooped him up, handed a biting, squawking, startled budgie back over the fence to me and I dropped him back in his cage. So miracles can occur.

Jim's ended up in the park around the corner from us. So long as he's within ear or eye shot there's hope.

Tim asks me to go home and get help from my other half, Cathy; she's always calm in a crisis. But the house is empty; she's still out shopping. I start walking around to the park, when Cathy suddenly appears in our car coming up the hill towards our house. When I tell her what's happened, she flies off to the park. I go back to the house and attempt to fix Tim's guitar. It starts to drizzle.

Cathy, Tim and Daniel march up our driveway then begin calling in our backyard. Jim's getting closer! He adores Tim, Tim adores him! Everywhere Tim goes, Jim goes. Jim came away to Port Fairy with us on our Christmas holidays; I'd see him in the rear-view mirror as he sat in his cage in the back seat of our car next to Tim. Cathy hid him in the closet of our holiday house when she discovered the landlady was going to come around and collect some blankets. You see, there was a no pets rule. We prayed the little bugger didn't squawk when the landlady small-talked to us. Jim comes with us sometimes when we visit my folks, who love cockatiels. Maybe the little fluff ball sees us as family. Who knows? Anyway, the feather brain is in our neighbour's gum tree just over the fence. Cathy reckons we should stop following him around and call from our house.

It's getting towards dusk now and I'm back inside drinking beer, doing my ironing. Drinking's the only way I can deal with this dreary chore; after a while, I don't care about the bloody creases. Daniel's gone home and Cathy and Tim are still out in the backyard calling to our fine feathered friend. When I told this story to my mum yesterday, she told me to hurry up, she couldn't stand the agony. So OK, this is what happened.

Tim came in at about six o'clock and as I was taking the clothes off the line, he broke down in his bedroom.

My heart heaved. 'Give it one more go,' I said to him and we joined Cathy out in the driveway.

It was still drizzling. Jim was on the power line at the end of our driveway. All three of us called to him. Daniel suddenly appeared in his folks' car; he'd forgotten his jumper. Cathy told him to stay in his car and got his jumper. Jim soared over our house! I started whistling, 'Pop goes the weasel'. Cathy called his name in a high-pitched friendly voice, and Tim held his arm up and did his special call that normally makes Jim land on him. Jim landed on the gumtree in our driveway and whistled back to us.

'You can see he wants to come back home,' Daniel's dad said from the car. He breeds rainbow finches, so he knows a thing or two about birds.

We kept calling and Jim landed on Cathy's shoulder. Tim walked up to his mother and held his arm up. Jim landed on him then Tim gently put him back in his cage. He carried it inside and we all broke down crying together. I kept stroking Tim's head to tell him I was proud of him and to never ever give up.

The strict rule now is never let Jim out when Tim's friend's come over, and he should only be let out to fly in his bedroom. Jim makes a jailbreak now and then. I complain about his poo in our lounge room when I vacuum.

What about the bird's perspective? My mum reckons Jim would have died. The bellbirds, the magpies or an owl would have got him. After all, how many escaped cockatiels do you see flying happily around the suburbs? Jim sees Tim as family. He frets whenever Tim's not around. He's fretting now; Cathy, Tim and Daniel have gone off to the pool. I'm trying to write this story while Jim is screaming in the lounge room. I've reluctantly let him out to spread his fluff and poo all over our house. He's now perched on his cockatiel play gym, preening himself in the golden sunlight. The little feathered gobshite!

Dust to Dust

The nine o'clock train bearing disturbed spirits hurtled towards the city; one of them was Christopher Kirkpatrick. The inner-suburban houses squeezed together like cramped passengers in a peak-hour carriage. The occasional European tree burnt in the morning sun, unlike the dark suburban forest that was his home. In the early hours of the morning, Christopher dreamed of a mud head, a wailing mud head, with a huge mouth and sad slits for eyes who lingered in a bog shrouded with grey light. It suffered from a great loneliness; Christopher felt its life flow through his body. His waking, crying soul struggled against the dream's despair. His wife Helen, and teenage son Will, had zoomed off to school. Christopher rubbed his teary blue eyes. Sunlight trickled into his bedroom. He felt like he'd been tossed up on a shore.

Christopher hesitated, but knew he had to drag his weary bones up to take a shower. The last time he stayed in bed he brooded too much and turned into a zombie. What the hell was that head about? Life's not bad at the moment, Christopher thought as he washed the shampoo from his thinning red hair.

Bitter experience taught him to deny his demons and keep plodding. But the head was no devil; it was pleading for something. He slowly shook his head, put on his everyday face and stepped through the front door. He had an open look which beggars and lost people approached in the city. Christopher flipped his hood on, stooped and like a stout medieval monk, made his way through the suburban forest drizzle. But he didn't have a crucifix to ward off the evil spirits. All he had was his sensitive soul.

The last time he'd wailed, he spiralled down into a nervous breakdown. It was during the middle of the day. Helen slapped his face and, like you see in Hollywood movies, it shut him up, but unlike the movies he kept crying inside.

Christopher chuckled to himself at the station with the realisation there was another time he moaned fairly regularly. It was during the early years of his marriage. Helen would rock him in her arms and stroke his sleep disturbed head. Again the cause of his tears was a dream but this one was more absurd than mud head. Flaring red or gold light would sail behind the living constellations of the night sky to settle in his backyard and then something would invade the newly weds' back door. Christopher would see bright lights but never saw who the creatures were. However, he was convinced they were aliens.

'Maybe you've been probed,' his serious-looking work colleague, Dianna McPhee, once told him after he revealed this silly dream to her.

What was equally strange was when he was having heart tests a few years ago, whenever the nurse ran the electronic hand-held thingamajig over his chest, the machine kept beeping. She couldn't figure it out and said, 'It's like you've got something metallic inside of you.'

'Maybe they've found the probe,' Helen laughed.

Christopher's train flew over the Yarra River. The city's unseasonable heat made him peel his coat off. To think that the early settlers used to say the river was silver. The last curling mists of dawn dissolved over the brown belly of the water. Rowers skimmed over its clay-coloured surface. In the early days, the Yarra used to be the dumping place for scores of factories and abattoirs. To this day, it's not a safe place to swim in; God knows what lurks below its murky waters now.

Any passenger observing Christopher staring out the window would probably dismiss him as a fairly average middle-aged codger, big-gutted, bald-headed with a silver beard. But his blue eyes betrayed him; they were always active. Our hero was usually lost in thought or reading a good novel. He was practically the last person left in the office to read a book. All the others either skimmed through rags like the *Herald Sun* or were lost in the drivel of an electronic screen. Christopher was one of those rare creatures who didn't have a mobile, was uninterested in iPhones, iPods, Facebook and big televisions. He was rereading Gogol, perhaps too much Gogol; *Diary of a Madman*, where the madman was convinced dogs talked and wrote. The Overcoat! The avenging ghost, who ripped the coats off people backs as they crossed the bridge in freezing St Petersburg.

'Probe!' Christopher tittered to himself as he walked through the baking hill end of Bourke Street. It was spring, but it was already like summer. The rising sun over Parliament House made him squint. The giant dome of the Exhibition building sat hazily below a powder-blue sky. One thought Christopher held was that, seeing we are made of clay, perhaps the rise in depression and various psychological ailments is reflective of how Mother Earth is feeling in this twenty-first century. The filth we've been pouring into the atmosphere for Christ knows how long has made her ill. She's warning us; every weather system on our blue planet is out of kilter.

UFOs: Christopher couldn't get over the similarity of these stories to ancient Celtic tales; strange lights, visitations in remote areas, abductions by pale creatures with large eyes and high cheekbones, visitations in remote areas, where times stands still et cetera. Are they signs of an anxiety we share with our ancestors? Yearnings for a better world? 'The majority of Yanks believe they've been abducted. Christ, they're a stupid race of people,' Christopher thought to himself. 'Surely Australians aren't so stupid? Hang on a minute: we've just voted in Tony Abbott as prime minister. The dropkick who's attempting to abolish the carbon tax through the smoke haze of too early spring bushfires. The trees of western Sydney's are sending the nation a message.

'I can still hear that clay head moaning in my mind. Have I moaned any time like that before my silly dreams?' Christopher asked himself. 'Yes,' came the reply from another voice inside his head. 'When you were born, like everybody else on this planet, you moaned when you realised you'd left your mother's womb.'

Christopher loved the view on the twentieth floor; you could see all the way back to the foothills of his home, which always seemed veiled in cloud. Grey clouds, purple thunder clouds, powder-white clouds, set against the backdrop of the blue Dandenong ranges. A view not straitened by mankind. It was always reassuring to know he'd return to this ever changing outskirt of town, teeming with nature; possums, bats and owls at night, magpies, butcher birds and corellas at day, just to name a few. He attempted to put mud head out of his thoughts, yet it still lingered in the background of his morning mood.

Christopher greeted his workmates with a chirpy gidday and opened up his first case. The plastic flowers a mother had ordered for her son's grave weren't the same ones she'd seen in the florist. Christopher took a deep breath and rang her to clarify things. It was her only son; he'd suffered a lifetime of bipolar disease and had tried numerous times to take his life. This time he had been successful. Christopher swallowed hard as he listened to her grief-stricken voice. The plastic flowers in the shop were a particular size and brightly coloured; the ones placed on her son's grave looked second-hand and smaller. She said the flowers were her final gesture for her son, and were ruined. When Christopher rang the florist, he was stunned by her officious voice; she didn't care, she was annoyed, maybe because she'd been caught out. Christopher negotiated a full refund. In an attempt to make the mother feel less isolated, he crossed the professional bounds of his job to tell her he'd been in a similar zone to her son and had learnt he had to keep moving. She thanked him.

Dianna came up to him and asked if he was all right.

'I just had a pretty sad case, that's all.'

Dianna's large green eyes moistened when he told her about his first case. His second case involved talking to a caravan park resident who had just got out of jail and was being illegally evicted by the park's manager. He rang the tenant to confirm a few things then, before he knew it was handed over to a policeman. Christopher told the senior constable that the manager didn't have a warrant. The policeman backed down. 'What hope do these people have, if they're treated like lumps of dirt when they get out?' Christopher asked himself.

The tenant's pleading voice reminded him of another man. He remembers sitting next to an angry passenger who almost came to blows with another standing passenger over the position of a backpack. The standing passenger dropped his backpack on the feet of the sitting passenger and made the mistake of aggressively telling him to move them. They eyeballed, swore and threatened each other. His neighbour apologised to Christopher after the standing passenger got off the train. The apology came straight from the heart. He said he'd been put in a boy's home when he was young. Christopher told him there was no need to apologise, because his grandfather was put in a home due to his mother no longer being able afford to look after him. Grandfather Alan, Christopher told the nodding passenger, never got over it. Alan was taken from his mother's house in Koo Wee Rup right across the other side of the state to Geelong when he was eight. He was stolen for four years and cried to himself every night. He told his grandson that the managers were brutes. 'Never forget when it comes to managers, Christopher, the shit always floats to the top.' Alan's anger always bubbled to the surface; he tended to blow up at the drop of a hat. He used to call his temper his 'Irish'. Christopher liked to think he hadn't inherited his grandfather's Irish.

Rain cascaded down the windows of his building as it creaked and groaned like a ship out at sea, then a patch of blue sky appeared. His leafy suburb was blanketed in thick silver cloud.

His third case involved chasing up a car dealer who was illegally keeping a young kid's deposit. The dealer moaned every time Christopher rang him up, complaining how he'd spent all morning arranging the deal, how much it had cost him. Christopher reminded him such were the hazards of the trade. The dispute had been dragging on for over a week now. The kid rang him practically every day. Christopher finally blasted the dealer into giving the money back.

Christopher and Dianna strolled along the shaded avenues of Treasury Gardens for lunch. They sat down on the grass below an oak tree near the J.F.K. Memorial. Christopher remembered being plonked in front of the television when he was four, his mother crying on the couch because 'they've just killed a good man'. He recalled the solemn music, the nightmarish image of Kennedy's exploding head. Christopher had a knot in his stomach. Dianna turned her fair head to him and asked if he was all right.

He was silent then said, 'I had this ridiculous dream last night, Di. With the medication I'm on, I don't usually recall my dreams, but this one…' He explained it to her. 'I've got no idea what it was about, but I felt incredibly sad, and haven't been able to shake the feeling off yet.' The irony was that he – Christopher Kirkpatrick – had, by any measure, a largely successful morning.

'Do you reckon the black dog's back?' Dianna was the only person he'd told in the office about his depression. They'd been working with each for well over twenty years.

'The black dog's always there, but I like to think he's on the leash.' Christopher looked down at the dry earth. He was on heavy-duty medication and drank too much. His excuse was that he had a demanding job and liked to drown his sorrows. Helen was forever trying to get him to cut down.

'I think the head is a part of you, Chris. It's coming from the core of your inner being. There's a great sadness there.' Dianna shifted her slim body into a more comfortable position beside the roots of the tree.

'Believe it or not, I like to think I'm not sad, Di, I'm coping. You know, I read somewhere we all have a negative voice inside of us. It's to do with evolution. Our ancestors always assumed the worst to survive, that's why they were so successful – they were prepared and it was a bonus if nothing bad turned out.'

Sunlight filtered through the tree; a hunchback seagull demanded food. Christopher threw him a few crumbs from his sandwich.

'But your dream was a message, Chris. It was powerful enough to wake you. Sounds like you're in denial.' A trickle of sunlight brushed Dianna's long blonde hair gold; her green eyes penetrated his blue.

'Denial! Denial's one of the best ways to deal with depression. After I was released from the hospital, I learnt not to dwell on it any more. I used to brood too much about what was causing me to fall apart. There's only so much personal history where you can blame your family, being bullied at school, boring work et cetera. Like Shakespeare says, "There's no good or bad only thinking makes it so." I did nothing but sit on my bed or pace. I couldn't even read any more, but that was something basic – my eyes were deteriorating due to the medication. Anyway, my dad bought a pair of reading glasses from the chemist. I put them on and I could read again. That was my first step back from the darkness. I don't deny the black dog, I've just thought of ways to tackle it. One of them's reading. It focuses my chattering mind.' Christopher sighed.

Thin white sheets of cloud drifted over the sun.

'Another way to tackle the black dog is to get on with life and try to ignore it, Di.'

'I'm a Celt, you're a Celt. We're a melancholy race. Just study our music and writing – it's all about dealing with loss. Maybe it's that simple. When Helen first met my family, she said she'd never met such melancholic people. We were grieving over Grandad. Maybe you never totally get over the death of a loved one.' Christopher patted his heart.

A furrow developed on Dianna's porcelain forehead. 'Chris, it's not that easy. There's a monster lurking in your unconscious that you have to acknowledge and deal with. My guess is that you're dissatisfied with your life and need to change it.' Dianna stared through him.

'Who's totally satisfied with his or her life? I've yet to meet them.'

It was one o'clock before they knew it. They stood and dusted themselves off. Christopher loved Dianna for her honesty. He knew she suffered from the same disease. Dianna had scars on her wrists and found it hard to sleep when the seasons changed. There are more people out there than we care to realise who suffer from psychological problems. All the old props are dying – God, rationality, socialism. The crass material emptiness of our existence is at its core. Everyone's competing for the latest and the best while our planet's heating up. Perhaps it's a matter of letting a fellow sufferer know that you're there for them, you'll listen, not judge and not preach.

During the afternoon, he worked on a case where he was caught a bankrupt estate agent trading illegally without a licence. The complainant groaned on about how this dodgy agent had been sitting on his money for months now. Christopher's heart raced when the director of the company threatened him legally. However, later on that day, he backed down and organised a full refund. Christopher referred the case to the legal section.

'My grandad used to say it was the simple things that make you happy. Nature's one of them,' Christopher declared to his drinking mates that night.

They all nodded. So did mud head when it rode the midnight train back to the suburban forest. Christopher grinned as the cicadas sang him off to sleep.

The following morning, he dreamt he was naked, drinking white wine outside below a caressing midday sun. He felt a warm inner glow in his stomach when he woke up. Like most dreams, it faded into the veils of twilight and was soon forgotten, except maybe by you dear reader.

Out of This World

Sally pointed to the distant mountains. 'The lights once came here when I was a little girl. When I say lights, they flew and hovered over the Western Tiers with searchlights.'

'Helicopters? What were they looking for?' I asked.

'No, they weren't helicopters, Alan,' Sally tittered, 'they were completely silent. There was no engine sound.' Sally rolled herself a cigarette.

We were sitting on the back porch of her farm.

She lit up, then plopped the tobacco pouch on my lap. 'It was in the papers back then. They were UFOs.' She blew her smoke up into the red-wine-coloured sky then smiled. 'Ah, dusk! It's my favourite time of day.'

'You're the first person I've ever spoken with who claims she's seen UFOs.'

A burning red summer sun sank behind the Western Tiers. The sky turned purple.

'Well, if you think about it, Alan, if you're travelling intergalactic, Dunorlan's a good place to change a spare tyre, especially back in the mid-sixties. There's nothing here but a tiny town and miles of wilderness.'

I was about to begin my last year of uni. I'd met Sally two years before. My mate Ross and I were both bored shitless with our jobs, so we quit and decided to hitchhike around Tasmania. Sally picked us up in her golden Land Rover just outside of Deloraine because we were walking around in 'bare feet'. Her philosophy was the less clothes the better. Ross and I had a fabulous week with her yarning, drinking, smoking a bit of dope and lots of laughter. Sally's farm, Madron, had no electricity or mod cons, but to Ross and me it was paradise. Sally was so free and easy. I can't remember any house rules. The King River backed onto her property and she and her friends used to bathe in it completely starkers.

My parents gave me some money when I turned twenty-one, so I decided to return to Madron.

'The Western Tiers were once tiger country, Alan. One story goes that after the death of the last one, years ago, a local farmer swears he saw a phantom tiger emerge from a cave then vanish before his very eyes. He christened the cave Tigerden. Who knows, it might have been a real tiger. My neighbour Pedley reckons he came across fresh droppings in the foothills just the other day.' Sally turned her deep green eyes towards me.

I studied the blue-vein deltas of her eyelids. I wasn't surprised by what Sally had told me. She and I have explored these anvil-shaped mountains numerous times. There's nobody within cooee. With its thick bushland of man ferns, waterfalls and ancient gums, it's a place where anything could happen.

'They found two lost children just outside the Tigerden after the lights disappeared, but they were different.' Sally took a deep drag on her cigarette.

'In what way?' I watched the last of the sun's rays dissolve into the now dark purple sky.

'They looked like any other boy or girl except they had green skin and were wearing clothes nobody had ever seen before.' Sally had a serious look on her face.

We'd become close over these few months on Modron. I like to think I knew when she was spinning me a yarn. Her green eyes would sparkle, a red rash would break out over her pale cheeks, then she'd pinch me on the bum. But this time she almost looked sad.

'What happened, Sal?'

'It was the same time as my birthday, when I turned eight. There was a huge kerfuffle in Dunlorlan. The police took them, but you see Pedley's such a powerful bastard – he has friends in high places in

Launceston. One day, the green girl reappeared on his farm. The boy, I later discovered, had died in custody. Imagine that: you have the freedom to roam thousands of light years from galaxy to galaxy, then you find yourself trapped with other boys in a home. Imagine the hell they would given him because of his colour. Boys' homes back then were run by fascists. Still are.' Sally stared up at the first star of twilight.

'The girl spoke in a tongue none of us understood. She'd shake her head every times Pedley's wife tried to feed her. I don't blame her. Iit was the traditional Anglo-Saxon fare of lamb, sausages, or any other variety of heavy red meat, terrible stuff. She was a vegetarian like me. After a while, they discovered the only food she could tolerate was beans. Her skin colour started to fade and she transformed into a young beauty with fiery red hair and skin so pale you could see every blue vein in her body.' Sally laughed when I said the girl sounded like her twin sister.

Sally told me she played with the alien girl, who was a tearaway, having no respect whatsoever for authority figures. (Probably because they caused the death of her brother.) She slowly mastered the English tongue and told Sally she came from a twilight planet where the sun never shone and lived in a domed city which floated on a silver lake. When their craft landed on the Western Tiers, their father told them not to stray, but children being children, they saw a dog-like creature with stripes on its back enter a cave. They raced after it, then became lost. After what seemed an eternity, they heard music coming from a small light in the distance. But as they stepped out of the cave, the fierceness of our sun dazzled them and the poor things collapsed onto the ground unable to move.

'It seems the music they heard came from the trannie of one of Pedley's sons. He was the one who discovered them paralysed and terrified. And so those UFOs were the parents looking for their lost children. The brightness of our sun was something they hadn't factored into the voyage. It would be very difficult to search for the kids coming from a world with no sun. I'll show you the newspaper cuttings, Alan.

I've still got them. You know what was curious, though, was that after the lights left the Western Tiers, there was a UFO report on the outskirts of Melbourne where a craft hovered over a primary school and terrified the kids. It then landed in a nearby field and the army showed up telling everyone to keep the incident a secret. Were the grieving parents contemplating kidnapping two of our kids?'

'What happened to the girl?'

'Oh, she's still around. Pedley set her up on a nearby farm.'

'Can I meet her? I mean, a woman from another world – she must have so many stories to tell.'

'You already have,' laughed Sally with a twinkle in her green eyes.

The stars were so bright that night that they seemed to sit on our shoulders. My head swam when I went to bed. I remember that report of a UFO hovering over a school. It was in a suburb called Westall, not far away from where I grew up. What the hell where they up to? I don't know how I'd react if I saw a UFO over the Western Tiers. Besides, here I was in the attic of Sally's house made of railway rafters, nodding off with an alien sleeping nearby.

This was just one of many stories Sally told me that summer thirty years ago, in the middle of nowhere on her farm in Tasmania. She said I was welcome to stay in Madron for as long as I liked. We kept in contact for a few years, writing to each other now and then. Her last letter talked about leaving Madron and going back home. I never heard from her after that. She just disappeared. I sometimes wonder what my life would have been like if I'd accepted her offer and not returned to university. Out of this world, I imagine.

A Journey To Glory

The still lough is silver, the three surrounding mountains dark blue. We're silently making our way back from St Kevin's, a grey twelfth century monastery. It's a pocket-sized church, with its still intact steep, stone roof, small round tower and conical top, nestled into the leafy shoulder of a nearby hill. This whole area of Ireland is a complex of monastic ruins.

'You can see why Kevin was happy to establish a hermitage here amongst the birds, clear water, rocks and pines. A sheltered more tranquil spot would be hard to find,' said my wife Kath.

I nod.

Man's been here a long time; some of these ruins were built over the graves and sacred spots of the pre-Christian clans. The early priests had to bend their teachings to accommodate the strong beliefs of the locals. Irish Christianity is merely one layer of belief over a people whose history stretches back to the Ice Age; they would have been here watching the glacier carve out Glendalough. Ireland is dotted with many Bronze Age or early Iron Age forts and stone rings. These people had a great reverence for the cycles of nature, the sky, land and water. They still do. You only have to walk around Glendalough or any other remote body of water in Ireland to know this is true.

My fifteen-year-old son Tim is starting to enjoy himself; he found the hustle and bustle of Dublin too much but now that he's walking through his first lush European forest, calm has entered his teenage body. Poor Tim, he's also missing his constant companion Jim, the cockatiel. Everywhere Tim goes, Jim goes on his shoulder. Jim was named after James T. Kirk, captain of the Star Ship *Enterprise*. Tim and I went through a big Star Trek stage, where I bought the entire early 1960s version and we'd spend long nights together watching episode after episode. Apart from the love of a good story, Tim has also inherited my deep love of nature. Even though he's fifteen, he still doesn't mind going bushwalking with his old man now and then on the weekends. My son has an encyclopaedic knowledge of the birds, animals and plants that inhabit the forests nearby our native city of Melbourne.

Tim squeaks with glee as he points to a nearby tiny brown wood mouse. The little fella suddenly leaves the main trail to scrabble up the rocky steps of a smaller path leading up a hill. We all decide to follow. The funny thing about this wood mouse is he's not scared of us as at all. He stays close, darting from one green hazelnut to another. The colour of his tiny eyes is as dark as the briquettes I used to haul into my family house when I was a boy.

Despite my blisters, we make it to the top and discover another church. This one's different; the roof's gone, perhaps a victim of the stupid Dublin English who sacked the whole area in 1398. Who knows? The flat-headed entrance portal still stands, so do the walls, which are held up by a series of round arches. There's an old green plaque on the side of the entrance which informs us that its name is Reefert Church. The word Reefert is an anglicised version of the original Gaelic Righ Fearta, which means burial place of kings. The plaque states that this was a royal burial ground before the coming of the Christians.

Tim leans over and chats to the wood mouse as I step through the entrance portal. Even though the roof has gone, the church still feels enclosed; the clear blue sky acts as a natural ceiling. There's a humbleness to the monasteries of Glendalough; they were constructed to blend into and not dominate the landscape. Kath shivers as she makes her way through the entranceway. The only sound is off our shoes as we crunch our way across the pebbled floor. I come across a long flat hole in the wall and peek in; it's full of coins and candles, an altar. Someone has placed a card in which reads, 'Life is not a race to the grave, but a journey to glory.' Righ Fearta after all these thousands of years is still a living place of worship!

I place some coins in and dedicate them to my Uncle Bernie Mullins, who died only a few weeks before our trip to the other side of the planet. Being a gentle soul, he should be at peace now in the Otherworld. Bernie always loved dancing. Years ago when my family had dos, all of us would end up dancing in our tiny weatherboard house which creaked and groaned under the pressure of scores of feet. Bernie would always be in the middle of the clan grooving away to the songs we teenagers would insist on playing, which was usually the Beatles. We've got a photo of him somewhere whistling while playing on his ukulele. Uncle Bernie was a fantastic whistler; he'd sometimes go all day. It's a dying art; you don't hear people whistling any more.

God, I miss those dancing, bouncing, house days! But like my uncle, I must keep myself open to the joy of existence, and travel's a good way of doing it. I nod to the altar, then make my way out of the church.

As Tim's little mate leads us back down the path, the hills and trees reflect like a mirror on the waters of Glendalough. We hear feral goats calling to each other and then a deer whistle high up on a hillside somewhere.

The ranger's hut is tucked away in the turning forest. Yellow leaves burst out of the green. We tell him about our little visitor then smile when he reckons it's unusual for a wood mouse to be out in the middle of the day and that they're usually weary of people. Thank you, little spirit, for giving me the opportunity to revere my uncle within such solitude.

I continue to light candles and give offerings to Bernie as we explore the grander churches of Europe, but there's nothing like Glendalough to remind you that, like an autumn leaf on a tree, you're a delicate part of a whole.

Somme Mist

It's a misty morning. The white sun smoulders behind a silver veil of cloud.

We're on the early morning train to Amiens, north of Paris. It's September 2014, a hundred years since the outbreak of World War I. Amiens is a town located in the battlefield known as the Somme. I'm about to fulfil a long held dream to visit my Great Uncle Edward's grave. He was killed in the battle of Mont St Quentin in September 1918.

When I was fourteen, my Pop, Thomas Cornell, gave me a gold medallion which belonged to his older brother, Edward; it was given when he volunteered back in 1916. It has the Australian coat of arms on it, surrounded by the words 'For King and Country'. On the back, the engraved words state, 'Presented by the residents of Mt Waverley to E. Cornell on enlisting for active service – 1916'.

Edward tried to volunteer with his brother Charlie when the war first broke out in 1914 but was rejected due to a chronic injury he'd sustained from pushing the plough. Edward was a market gardener and worked on the Cornells' family farm in the now suburban Mount Waverley. He was devastated when Charlie sailed off without him. But in 1916 with a huge casualty rate and declining number of volunteers, the authorities weren't as strict as before when it came to health standards, and Edward was allowed to join.

I'll never forget Pop polishing the medal before he gave it to me; he had a tear in his eye as he told me Edward was his favourite brother and was a gentle soul. I treasure the medal and have worn it off and on for forty years now. Edward had it with him when he died. I have an official document that records Edward's personal effects shipped back to Australia after his death; it mentions the medallion. I wonder if it was on the sweetheart's chest when his heart stopped beating? My Great Auntie Alice died when I was nineteen; she was close to Edward, lived in the Cornell family home and never married. I read somewhere that the trauma of the death of a loved one in the Great War flows through the blood of the succeeding generations. Pop made it a point to hand over to me a small cardboard box Alice had kept for sixty years. It contained Edward's medals, photos, documents, letters, and handmade silk postcards sent back from France. I read everything straight away. There's letters from his chaplain and friends which tell of how he died. Edward and another soldier were carrying a wounded officer down Mont St Quentin when they were hit by German artillery. The other soldier was killed instantly (I suspect the officer was too). Edward was badly wounded on the side of his body and head, and died on the operating table.

I rub my eyes as we step off the train at Amiens; we've been up since five-thirty. The mist has lifted and it's a beautiful sunny day. Our tour guide, Barbara, rocks up in a mini-van with a large Australian flag emblazoned on the side; her company is called True Blue Tours. When Barbara introduces herself, she instantly strikes me as larger than life, generous, and with a passion for World War I. She tells us that the war was the greatest disaster in the two thousand year history of Western civilisation. She gets no argument from my wife Kimberly or fifteen-year-old son Thomas. I reply, 'You're not wrong, Barbara.'

Barbara takes us to Amiens Cathedral, which is still intact despite two world wars and the burning of the township. They've only just finished cleaning off the smoke stains from World War II! The cathedral is identical in style to Notre Dame. Barbara tells us it's the largest Gothic church in France. She takes us to a plaque which expresses gratitude to the Australian, New Zealand and American armies who defended the city between March and April at the height of the Germans' 1918 offensive. We're then shown a statue up in the rafters of a weeping angel. It represents that moment in life when we discover in our childhood that death is going to take us all away. I remember that moment when I was about seven on summer holidays with Pop and Nana down in Rosebud. I was devastated and cried all night. I couldn't handle the fact that one day Nana and Pop weren't going to be here any more. Barbara tells us the statue was a favourite of the soldiers before they went off to the Western Front. I realise Edward would have seen it.

Barbara tells us our next destination is the village of Villers-Bretonneux. As we drive through the vast flat brown fields of the Somme, I realise how you would have been seen for miles around by your enemy as you stumbled across no-man's-land – there was no cover or escarpments. It's no wonder they dug trenches. Barbara pulls the van up and points to a forest-covered hill on the outskirts of Villers-Bretonneux. We step into the warm embracing French sunshine.

Barbara's knowledge of our troops astounds me. You hear all these stories that the French don't like foreigners and are quite aloof. We've been in France for days and neither Kim, Tom nor I have experienced any of that nonsense.

Barbara tells how hundreds of Australian soldiers hid up there on Anzac Eve 1918. 'Now up until Anzac Day, the Germans had been on the offensive for thirty-five days, sweeping the British army before them. The Germans had negotiated an armistice with the Russians in December 1917. As a result, they had a million more soldiers to throw into the conflict on the Western Front. They hoped to smash the Allies before the American reinforcements arrived in France. They were well on the way to doing that until the Australians hiding in the forest on top of that hill joined in on the conflict.'

I'd read about these men and how when they marched to the front they tried to convince the retreating British to join them, but it didn't happen. However, when the fleeing villages saw them, they shouted to each other, 'The Australians are here,' and returned to their homes.

'Now picture this,' Barbara said. 'Two exhausted brigades yet they were determined because it was the third anniversary of Anzac Day. They attack in the early morning darkness without artillery support and catch the Germans completely by surprise. They capture the village and take a thousand prisoners. It was the first setback of the Germans' 1918 offensive and it was your countrymen who did it!'

'Another Australian military victory that goes largely unrecognised,' my American-born wife Kimberly states.

We enter the heart of the village and Barbara takes us to the Victoria School. It has a plaque out front which states,

> THIS SCHOOL BUILDING IS THE GIFT OF THE SCHOOL CHILDREN OF VICTORIA AUSTRALIA TO THE CHILDREN OF VILLERS-BRETONNEUX AS A PROOF OF THEIR LOVE AND GOOD WILL TOWARDS FRANCE. TWELVE HUNDRED AUSTRALIAN SOLDIERS THE FATHERS AND BROTHERS OF THESE CHILDREN GAVE THEIR LIVES IN THE HEROIC RECAPTURE OF THIS TOWN FROM THE INVADERS OF 24th APRIL BURIED NEAR THIS SPOT. MAY THE MEMORY OF A GREAT SACRIFICE IN A COMMON CAUSE KEEP FRANCE AND AUSTRALIA TOGETHER FOREVER IN BONDS OF FRIENDSHIP AND MUTUAL ESTEEM.

Surely Thomas Cornell would have given a few quid to this school, I think. There's a large sign out in the main playground which says,

> NEVER FORGET THE AUSTRALIANS.

As soon as we step into the school hall we immediately smell the scent of Australian wood.

'Oh, Barbara, this smell is distinctly Australian. It reminds me of an old hall built up in the Dandenong Ranges just before World War I. I can smell the resin in the timber. It's such a unique smell,' Kimberly smiles.

'That's amazing, Kimberly, because this wood was shipped from Australia to build the school. I think it's called Australian maple. It makes me so happy to know that you pick up the scent of Australia in a hall in France. It makes me feel that it's more Australian,' Barbara replied.

The wooden hall's timber has a golden brown sheen to it. Kim's right. I remember Auntie Alice's house had the same scent. Up on top of the school walls are beautiful carvings of our unique animals. We make out a possum, a lyre bird, a platypus, a cockatoo and, as a Collingwood supporter, I'm glad to say that there's a carving of a magpie with his wings proudly stretched out.

This is my first visit to a non-English-speaking country. I have overlooked the reverence the people here have for my countrymen. All Australians have forgotten! We focus on the great tragedy of Gallipoli. But compared to the Western Front, Gallipoli was a sideshow. Not to mention that once we gained an Australian commander on the Western Front, John Monash, our men won a series of victories. Why aren't these achievements celebrated as much as Anzac? 'Australian's don't blow their own trumpet like other countries,' Kimberly once told me. Well, in this increasing age of digitalisation, US cultural imperialism and negativity, there's even more of a need to get our stories out there.

Just before lunch, Barbara takes us to a field full of shell holes. We stop on the side of the road to look into a pocket of forest and, sure enough, below the trees we see scores of overgrown craters.

'How come the local farmers don't get rid of them, Barbara?' I ask.

'Because there's too many of them. The farmers prefer to let them be.'

It's an unearthly vision, a pockmarked field like the moon; despite being overgrown with ivy, you can still make out the circular shapes. Even after a hundred years, you get an idea of the destruction the shells wrought. I've had my mind on Edward all day, the artillery he and his mate caught! I slowly shake my head from side to side.

Barbara takes us to a local French restaurant; the first thing I order is a beer. She tells us about Monash's first battle as corps commander of the Australian army. Where he constructs a giant replica of Hamel and its surroundings and, through a series of talks, advises his troops to familiarise themselves with the objectives of the upcoming battle. Something like this had never taken place on the Western Front before. Most of the British commanders saw themselves as far too superior to associate with their troops. Another radical step Monash took was to familiarise his troops with tanks. They were reluctant because the machines were useless at Bullecourt. They either broke down or got bogged and left our men exposed to withering German fire. However, Monash, through a series of drills which took place for weeks, got his men used to them. Some of the diggers adopted a tank and wrote pet names on them.

I order a meal and another beer and listen to this amazing French woman who has such a reverential knowledge of my countrymen.

'On 4 July, a heavy mist, unusual for summer, descended onto the battlefield. Monash used artillery and planes to smother the sound of the sixty tanks making their way up to the front. Just before dawn each morning preceding the battle, he'd shot off a series of coloured smoke bombs to give the impression they were shooting off mustard gas. It worked. The Germans were forced to wear gas masks, which restricted their vision and movement. Then on 4 July the tanks suddenly emerged from the smoke and mist only metres away from the Germans front line. The Diggers themselves were a quicker and more mobile force than before, because they didn't have to wear packs. The Diggers obtained their supplies from planes and tanks. The days of slow pack mules were over. The enemy's front line was shattered within seconds. Monash had calculated that if it went to plan, the battle it would take ninety minutes. He was wrong: it took ninety-three minutes. In that small amount of time, Monash accomplished what other British commanders had never achieved. Don't forget, some commanders had pushed their troops for months to gain a few metres. After the Battle of Hamel, the commanders of the Allied Armies ordered the generals to adopt Monash's tactics. They did and the Germans were pushed back. So it was your commander John Monash who was responsible for turning the tide of the war. You Australians should be aware of this. Hamel was a major victory for the Allies and was the beginning of the end for the Germans.' Barbara sipped her mineral water.

We three were stunned. I'd read a lot about the war, had a

knowledge of Monash. But I suppose I'm a victim of a widespread belief that the Western Front was a tragedy, ebbing into the grey mists of time. We all have images of slow straight lines of soldiers being massacred by the machine gun. Nothing positive came out of that war, but here was a soldier from the Antipodes who had figured out how to defeat the Germans without sending thousands of young men into certain slaughter. One of his maxims was 'industrial protection'; in other words, protecting men as much as possible, with tanks, planes, creeping artillery, smoke bombs, anything to reduce casualties. I reflect on how tragic it was that nobody in Australia knew this heroic story. Monash was knighted by Edward VI after Hamel, and was seriously considered to take over command from that great nincompoop, Field Marshal Douglas Haig. But two things in the jaundiced eye of the British establishment stood against him: he was a colonial and, perhaps even worse, he was Jewish.

Nowadays, kids wrap themselves up in flags, paint flags on their faces, and shed tears at dawn on the beaches and cliffs of Gallipoli. However, the pilgrimage should begin in Gallipoli and continue through the Western Front towards the eventual defeat of the once-powerful German Army. Our young men were in the thick of it; sometimes the number killed in Gallipoli was equalled in one day of fighting in France until Monash took command.

We buy a small wooden cross with a poppy on it and a small Australian flag at Villers-Bretonneux and bear them to Edward's grave. I've inherited old black and white photos of his grave and can't believe Barbara is taking us to his military cemetery of Hem Farm. I keep swallowing; my stomach's been in my throat all day. I think of Pop, of Nana, who I promised just before her death that if I ever had a son I'd call him Thomas.

Barbara pulls her True Blue van up in the tiny village of Feullières and there it is: a quiet, square little cemetery next to a farm. Tom and I jump out and march through it with a copy of a map kept by Aunty Alice. Kimberly films us. We find Edward's humble grave straight away, below a white rectangular piece of stone. I keep placing kisses upon his headstone as I talk to him. I introduce myself as Tom's grandson then introduce our Tom. We promise never to forget him. All three of us sit down next to his grave and talk to him until we all become tearful.

The gravestone tells how he died age thirty at the battle of Mont St Quentin. He fought with the Twenty Second Battalion Australian Infantry. One of his officers when writing back to Edward's parents called Mont St Quentin 'that most impregnable fortress'. It had been held by the Germans for four years, bristling with barbed wire, fortifications and machine gun nests. The Twenty Second had been fighting non-stop for seventy-two hours when they took the decision to storm the mount. The Germans were caught completely by surprise and chased off the battlefield. Some historians claim it was the most heroic battle of World War I.

Edward's parents had placed the words 'Our darling Ted, he died for us' on Edward's gravestone. So they called him Ted! Charlie had a son christened Edward, but we all knew him as Uncle Ted. Uncle Ted fought in World War II for six years without a scratch. I helped him write his biography before he died, but that's another story. I take a handful of stones from Edward's grave for my dad. Barbara subtly shifts the mini-van, we wipe our eyes, then Tom promises Edward that he'll bring his family back to visit him. For some unknown reason, I shout a cooee as we leave the cemetery. Kim and Tom do a cooee as well.

We write in the visitor's book (it's full of loving words from many families around Australia) and, as we get back into her True Blue van, Barbara tells us the visitors books and cemeteries on the Western Front have never been vandalised.

Barbara takes us to our last stop, Mount St Quentin. It's a high hill. Barbara tells us it got the name from an Irish monk St Quentin, who built a monastery on top of the hill in the sixth century. I smile as Barbara tells us that a number of place names in France are named after Irish monks who came to France after the collapse of the Roman

Empire. These brave men were seen as the torch-bearers for Western civilisation, for they brought not only the teachings of Christ but also the wisdom of ancient Rome and Greece. One of the reasons I'm smiling is that my mother's side of the family are Irish. The first place we visited in Europe was Ireland, and we're still basking in the glow of a wonderful trip. I wonder if Edward knew there was an Irish monastery on top of the mount he was charging, and was he taken into St Quentin's care?

The ugly reality was that a pillbox for German artillery stood on top of the hill. The men in that box would have directed the shellfire that killed Edward. The Twenty Second Battalion was ordered to shout like bushrangers as they charged up the hill. I can't help but think some of them would have shouted out cooees. I wonder if this order came directly from Monash? As a young boy, he met Ned Kelly at Jerilderie. The bushranger was said to have given him some good advice. Monash never revealed what it was, but said his meeting with Ned was one of the highlights of his life, and speculated on what great soldiers the Kelly gang would have made.

A large statue of an Australian soldier now stands high on the peak of Mont St Quentin. I imagine a khaki horde of yelling, screaming soldiers storming up this hill. I can see them cutting barbed wire, shooting, bayoneting, throwing hand grenades at German machine guns. Yet Edward's last act was to try to rescue a fellow soldier. His last vision would have been coming down this hill, burdened by the weight of an unconscious officer. I wonder if we have managed to communicate with him somehow. With his body in the womb of French soil, did he hear our voices? After death, is it possible to share an experience with your blood relative? The crying angel in the cathedral tells me it is. So does the Somme sun and mist. So does my vision of Mont St Quentin. I can't help but think Edward lived all of his life on a mount, then was killed coming down one in France.

Unfortunately, Barbara has to rush us back to Amiens. She plays military music on the way. 'Advance Australia Fair' comes on. Barbara senses that I can't stand it then plays 'Waltzing Matilda', which sends shivers up and down my spine. We give each other hurried kisses and hugs and run for the train at Amiens.

It's now dusk, the bloated sun is red. As I leave the Somme, I can hardly see anything. The light's blinding, the carriage is red, the surrounding land is red. The mist returns to caress the battlefield with her moist fingers and transform our train into a shadow.

Back home, my mother nods when I tell her it was a very spiritual day. My frail father acknowledges the stones as I place them in his palm.